Kidnapped!

"Get out," said Ms. Slaight.

There was something in her voice. Worse than before. Worse than ever before.

My fault, Marnie thought. My fault.

Marnie got out. She would rather walk anyway.

But Ms. Slaight got out, too. She grasped Marnie's arm and forced her away from the car. She looked down into Marnie's face, and her expression was like nothing Marnie had ever seen before. It hypnotized her. As if from a distance, she could hear Ms. Slaight speaking.

"I didn't want it to be this way between us, Marnie Skyedottir. But from the very first time I met you, I think I knew that it would have to be." And she raised her other hand. There was something in her clenched fist.

Marnie later remembered everything else, but not the actual feel of the sharp blow to her head.

OTHER BOOKS BY NANCY WERLIN

LOCKED INSIDE

NANCY WERLIN

speak
An Imprint of Penguin Group (USA) Inc.

For Maxwell Romotsky

*Everyone should be lucky enough
to have an Uncle Max*

SPEAK
Published by the Penguin Group
Penguin Group (USA) Inc., 345 Hudson Street, New York, New York 10014, U.S.A.
Penguin Group (Canada), 90 Eglinton Avenue East, Suite 700, Toronto, Ontario, Canada M4P 2Y3
(a division of Pearson Penguin Canada Inc.)
Penguin Books Ltd, 80 Strand, London WC2R 0RL, England
Penguin Ireland, 25 St Stephen's Green, Dublin 2, Ireland (a division of Penguin Books Ltd)
Penguin Group (Australia), 250 Camberwell Road, Camberwell, Victoria 3124, Australia
(a division of Pearson Australia Group Pty Ltd)
Penguin Books India Pvt Ltd, 11 Community Centre, Panchsheel Park, New Delhi - 110 017, India
Penguin Group (NZ), 67 Apollo Drive, Rosedale, North Shore 0632, New Zealand
(a division of Pearson New Zealand Ltd)
Penguin Books (South Africa) (Pty) Ltd, 24 Sturdee Avenue, Rosebank, Johannesburg 2196, South Africa

Registered Offices: Penguin Books Ltd, 80 Strand, London WC2R 0RL, England

First published in the United States of America by Delacorte Press, 2000
Published by Speak, an imprint of Penguin Group (USA) Inc., 2009

3 5 7 9 10 8 6 4 2

Library of Congress Cataloging-in-Publication Data
Werlin, Nancy.
Locked inside / Nancy Werlin.
p. cm.
Summary: After she is kidnapped from the exclusive boarding school
she attends, heiress Marnie Skyedottir must rethink her idealized relationship
with her mother, her own sense of who she is, and her relationships with others.
ISBN 978-0-14-241374-6 (paperback)
[1. Self-perception—Fiction. 2. Identity—Fiction.
3. Mothers and daughters—Fiction. 4. Kidnapping—Fiction.] I. Title.
PZ7.W4713Lo 2009
[Fic]—dc22
2008024293

Speak ISBN 978-0-14-241374-6

Printed in the United States of America

What other dungeon is so dark as one's own heart!
What jailer so inexorable as one's self!

—*Nathaniel Hawthorne,*
The House of the Seven Gables

CHAPTER I

At sixteen years of age, Marnie Skyedottir had a personal net worth of $235.27 million. That she made do on $50 a week was the work of Marnie's guardian, Max Tomlinson, and Marnie knew that one day—on her twenty-first birthday, to be exact—she could, if she chose, have revenge.

"I'll fire your sanctimonious butt, Max," she told her computer screen, where a characteristically lengthy and courteous e-mail from Max lay open. (. . . *As you know, the regulations for Halsett Academy for Girls clearly stipulate that students on academic probation should not have access to excess personal funds. . . .*) Marnie could almost hear Max speaking the words in his Mississippi lawyer's drawl that, for all its leisured pace, somehow never sounded any less than definite.

"Your years managing my life will be over"—she

jabbed at the keyboard with satisfaction and precision—"like that."

Max's e-mail disappeared into the Trash. Marnie blinked and only then realized her eyes hurt. Burned. And her shoulders ached. She flexed them, and shut her eyelids tightly for a few seconds. Well, no wonder she was in pain. Before the reply from Max had arrived, she'd been online for a while, chasing that clever, thieving, infuriating Elf through the dark winding virtual alleys of Upper Paliopolis. She glanced down at the clock on her computer. 5:43 A.M. Max was up early in New York City, in that huge duplex apartment on Central Park West that Marnie was supposed to call home. Ha.

Wait. 5:43 A.M.?

"No!" Marnie moaned instinctively, and then clapped a hand over her mouth. Dorm walls weren't very thick. But it couldn't be. She couldn't have been online for over ten hours! She directed a fierce glare at the clock, as if she could will it to spin backward to, say, 10 P.M. Early enough for her to go over her chem notes and then go to bed at midnight, like a good preppy Halsett girl—like Jenna Lowry or Tarasyn Pearce or someone like that.

Instead the clock went forward. 5:44 A.M. And her computer beeped as words appeared in the Paliopolis chat window. A message from that pesky Elf glowed neon in the dark of Marnie's room.

Giving up? The sneer was implicit.

Marnie hesitated. She disliked her chemistry class with its brooding, angry teacher, and she wasn't doing well in it. There was no chance of sleep now, but

2

if she at least spent an hour with the notes, maybe she could pass the test today.

Thanks for the spellbook, Sorceress, the Elf gibed. *You'll be a lot more helpless without it. I'm looking forward to watching your rating plummet. While mine soars!* The message was accompanied by a belching raspberry noise; Paliopolis sound effects were crude but effective.

Well, who needed sleep? The Elf had been on just as long as Marnie, and if he could keep going, so could she. Or rather, so could her alter ego, the Sorceress Llewellyne. It was not for nothing that Llewellyne had the highest player rating in all of Paliopolis.

Marnie grinned and attacked the keyboard. *Dream on, you drooling nitwit,* she typed to the Elf.

She had more than two hours before she had to be in class, anyway.

The chemistry test was straight from the book; the kind that anyone who had read over her notes could have passed easily. Marnie amused herself by drawing nooses and happy faces wherever she didn't have a clue. It only took a couple of minutes. Inspired, she then added two tiny mice in chains next to the final question regarding the nature of covalent bonds, and had difficulty suppressing a fit of exhausted giggles. A chuckle escaped anyway. Marnie didn't need to look up to see the teacher's sharp glance. She could feel it.

"Something funny, Ms. Skyedottir?" At Marnie's shoulder, Ms. Slaight carefully enunciated each absurd syllable of Marnie's last name. Marnie could feel the sudden alert attention of the entire class. Ms. Slaight reached down and plucked up Marnie's test to scan. "You're not Picasso," said Ms. Slaight finally. Not even a glimmer of amusement could be found on her face. "I assume you're done?"

"My artistic vision is exhausted," said Marnie blithely. "Take it away." Then she realized her left hand was embedded in her hair, twisting nervously. She pulled the hand down. She was not going to let Ms. Slaight, of all people, rattle her. She watched as the teacher took her red pen and marked a big *F* at the top of her test.

"Back to work, people," said Ms. Slaight. She was holding her thin shoulders tensely. "Ms. Skyedottir's little display is over." The class sank again into the test, and Marnie watched Ms. Slaight return to her own desk.

The chemistry teacher was thirtyish; a term substitute who had taken over the class at the beginning of the semester when the regular teacher went on maternity leave. Marnie had heard this was her first actual teaching job. That might explain her defensive jitteriness in the classroom, and possibly also the pathetic, pieced-together wardrobe. Today, for example, she was wearing scuffed black pumps, a dull brown skirt, and a lime-green bow blouse.

Discomfort with teaching might also explain the controlled, but very present, edge to Ms. Slaight's voice whenever she spoke to Marnie. Not to mention the way Ms. Slaight always pronounced Marnie's last name, so carefully, so distinctly. Okay, it was a ridiculous name; embarrassing even if, by some miracle, you had never heard of Marnie's mother. Skye had been inspired by Icelandic naming conventions, and Marnie could only be relieved she hadn't taken things further. Cirrus Skyedottir. Thunder Skyedottir. Asteroid Skyedottir. Oh, Marnie had a long mental list of first names she might have had, if Skye—who had been cheerfully capable of anything—hadn't exercised rare restraint.

Skye.

Even on all the legal contracts that defined her small empire of recordings, books, and financial dealings, Marnie's mother had been simply Skye. She had cut her birth name from her life so completely that none of the media types had ever been able to discover who she really was, or where she'd come from. Marnie often wondered about these same questions, even though she knew that Skye would have said grandly that it did not matter.

The self you invent, Skye had written, *the self you live by—that is the self who is important. You are who you choose, consciously or unconsciously, to be. It is better to be conscious. It is better to take control.* That was from her first bestseller, *Inventing Your Soul.*

In fact, to Marnie's knowledge, Skye had never talked—either to Marnie or publicly—about her life before she got her first recording contract at twenty-one. Marnie knew absolutely nothing about Skye's parents or her childhood. She didn't know if Skye had had brothers and sisters, uncles and aunts, grandparents. For all Marnie knew, Skye had magically appeared in the world at twenty-one, fully grown, singing solo in a church choir in . . . actually, Marnie didn't even know exactly where it was that the record producer had first heard Skye. Georgia? Mississippi, where Max was originally from? Marnie knew that Max's relationship with Skye—more than friends, less than lovers, far more complicated than employee with employer—went way back. It dated from before the time that Skye had hired Max to handle all her myriad legal affairs, from long before Marnie's birth.

Yes, Max certainly knew more about Skye than Marnie did. Three years ago she had asked him directly about Skye's past. It had been in the middle of her birthday dinner with him and the housekeeper, so he couldn't escape. He had looked intently at Marnie for several seconds, his face unreadable, and Marnie had dared to hope. But then he had said with uncharacteristic brevity, "One day," and changed the subject. Marnie had ignored his and Mrs. Shapiro's attempts to draw her into the conversation, had put down her fork and fumed.

But from that day, her desire to know had warred with the opposite feeling. Marnie was no fool. Skye would not have concealed, not have run from, a happy past. And the lack of expression on Max's face told its own tale.

Perhaps it had been then—and not at Skye's death—that she had begun to feel the deep fear.

Now Marnie slumped in her chair and waited, unthinking, for the bell and release. She had the beginnings of a headache. It was lack of sleep. Only that.

She blamed the Elf. Before he came online, she used to play for only two or three hours a night.

Ms. Slaight worsened the headache immediately after class. "I have English," Marnie said to her. "Can't we do this later?" But she wasn't surprised when the peculiar teacher merely pointed, silently, at the chair next to her desk. Marnie sat down sideways, on the edge. Then, as Ms. Slaight spoke, Marnie mouthed the words just a breath behind her. She'd heard it all recently, from other teachers. Ms. Slaight was not very original. And she spoke almost robotically, as if she'd memorized the little speech from a book on teaching methods.

You're not trying. You're a smart girl, clearly able to do the work. I'm willing to hear about any personal problems. I would like to help. We can arrange a conference. . . .

Marnie didn't say anything, and Ms. Slaight got more and more angry, even offended. "Look at me!" she exclaimed finally. Marnie did so, with her best blank face. Ms. Slaight had gotten quite red. She was practically spitting. Marnie wondered, idly, if you could have a heart attack when you were only around thirty, or if you had to spend decades working yourself into fits first.

"Marnie Skyedottir," Ms. Slaight said. Again she leaned viciously on Marnie's last name. "You really think you're someone."

Marnie stilled. Then her tired mind replayed the exact way the chemistry teacher had pronounced *Skyedottir* just now, and a bitter taste filled her mouth. At once Ms. Slaight made sense. All this rage was somehow aimed at Skye. This was a person

7

who had found Skye—her idiosyncratic belief system, her writings and speeches, her wealth and success, her oddities, her flaunted fatherless daughter—personally offensive. There were such people. Max had a whole file cabinet filled with old hate mail. Marnie had once overheard him speaking with Mrs. Shapiro about it.

Marnie discovered her fists were clenched. She might criticize Skye herself sometimes, in the far reaches of her own head, but that anyone else should dare!

"In this world," Ms. Slaight had gone on, "you'll find that princessy behavior will get you precisely nowhere. In this world, an attitude like yours—"

Marnie stood up and, startled, Ms. Slaight stopped speaking. Marnie looked her right in the eye. In a heartbeat, several possible things to say flashed into her mind. What she, Marnie *Skyedottir*, thought of creepy skinny ugly chemistry teachers and *their* attitudes. The fact that she, Marnie *Skyedottir*, was rich (or would be) and Ms. Slaight wasn't and *that* was what the world cared about, not chemistry tests. That Ms. Slaight needed to get a life, quick, because the one she had right now was a pretty sorry excuse. In the opinion of Marnie *Skyedottir*.

She did not say any of these things. Instead, she carefully turned her head to the side, presenting Ms. Slaight with a full view of her right cheek. Then, as carefully, and smiling, she turned her face the other way, showing the other cheek.

Matthew 5:39.

Ms. Slaight got it. She gasped. Marnie coolly brushed past her and walked out of the classroom. She even made it to English on time. That would have made her laugh if, underneath it all, she hadn't been so angry.

It wasn't important, she tried to tell herself. People like Ms. Slaight were not important. Skye would say . . . well.

Actually, Skye would not approve. Skye would say that Marnie had misapplied Matthew.

But then, Skye had never been Skye's daughter.

Marnie took in a calming breath. She would not think about it. She would not.

Tonight she would track down the Elf and get back her spellbook. He'd be online; he always was lately. In fact, he'd been teasing her, or rather, the Sorceress, very particularly for a few weeks now. It was time to crush him for his impertinence.

Maybe in the tunnels below the city? Marnie knew Paliopolis better than anyone except its programmers and the Dungeon Master, and even without her spellbook, she had a trick or ten.

As her English teacher drew a triangular diagram of a well-constructed essay on the white board, Marnie planned her evening, mentally mapping out the tunnels and sewers and traps and dangers of the cyberspace world of Paliopolis. The Elf had the overconfidence of a lucky newbie. And okay, he was a little smart, too. But that didn't matter. If she didn't get him in the next few days, she'd get him next week during spring break. She'd said no to Max about going home to New York, and so she'd be right here at school. She'd have long uninterrupted hours available to go online.

The Elf had better watch out.

CHAPTER 2

This year, eleventh grade, was Marnie's fifth year of boarding school, but she had never become accustomed to the communal meals. It wasn't the food—if there wasn't something edible served, you could always have salad, or toast with peanut butter. No, it was all the people. There was always someone looking at her, even after all this time at the school. People never stopped looking, covertly, at Skye's daughter. Marnie used to wonder what they were hoping to see. That had been one reason why, when she was fourteen, she'd chopped off most of her hair and then bleached the rest white as dandelion fluff. With the careful half-inch of dark at the roots, it screamed fake. Marnie loved it. It gave the gawkers something real to talk about; something that was her choice. On top of that, any time she got really scared, really shy, she'd paint huge circles of black eyeliner around her eyes. If she also put on her favorite neon pink T-shirt—far more noticeable than black—and her entire collection of heavy silver rings and chains, she could face just about anyone.

Marnie's first boarding school—her first school, in fact, because before that Skye had taught Marnie at home—had been a bigger, coed institution, with a cafeteria. Marnie had looked ordinary then, except for the shocking resemblance to Skye. In that cafeteria, she had had to walk through the press of tables that were full of other kids, teachers, and the occasional headmaster or dean before she could finally get into line with a tray. She'd felt everyone watching her back while she went through the line. Then, when she'd finally emerged with food, she'd had to turn and survey the sea of faces again, looking for a table at which she could reasonably sit and eat.

It didn't help that there were at least a dozen other "celebrity" kids at that first school. Their parents were famous actors or corporate titans or rock stars. Whereas Skye was an ex-gospel singer who'd started her own . . . well, some said it was practically a religion. Suffice it to say that Skye was not the same kind of celebrity parent that those other kids had.

Strange, was what the other kids called Marnie. Maybe it was true. Marnie suspected that there was more to strangeness than the dictionary would have you think. As Skye had often said, *If you want things to be simple, sweetheart, you should go ahead and end it all right now.* Which was not typical advice, Marnie now knew, to give to your daughter when she—for example—complained about long division.

The feeling of being watched always came back at mealtimes.

Halsett Academy for Girls, located in semirural Halsett, Massachusetts, near the New Hampshire border, did not have a cafeteria. Instead, there was a rather pretty Victorian dining hall, with floral wallpaper and tables of dark wood at which you had an assigned place. Initially, Marnie had thought this a better system. But you could always leave a cafeteria, while here, during dinner, you had to sit for a full hour, passing platters under the eyes of the staff. Marnie hadn't decided if it was better or worse now that, because she was an upperclasswoman, her table was free of a permanent, assigned supervisor.

This evening, Marnie came to dinner at the last possible moment—she'd have skipped the meal if it wouldn't have stirred up more trouble than she wanted to deal with just now—because she'd been putting the finishing touches on her plan to confound the Elf. Even now, as she slipped into the last available chair at her table, she was still thinking about it. She'd had one idea after another, fountaining, all afternoon. She nodded a vague hello to the table of girls and quickly bowed her head for grace.

Grace at Halsett Academy was a gentle melody with inoffensive, nondenominational lyrics. (*Might as well sing to your big toe, if you're not going to bother even mentioning God,* Skye would have said.) Marnie didn't join in, but she didn't mind listening, either. Some of the girls had nice voices. Jenna Lowry had a clear soprano; Tarasyn Pearce a powerful alto, almost a tenor. Tarasyn's voice had actually shocked Marnie the first time she'd heard it, so similar was it to Skye's. But here in the dining hall, it was muted somewhat by the other voices, including a couple that could have flattened small hills. Marnie herself, for reasons she'd never bothered to investigate, had never done more than mouth the words. She just didn't care to sing publicly, she had explained early in the year. She knew they'd probably thought she'd inherited Skye's voice. Ha.

The song ended, and the bustle of the meal began. Barb Schulman asked for the butter and Marnie passed it over, for the first time looking up fully and seeing—Mrs. Fisher. Mrs. Fisher, dorm counselor, was sitting two tables away with a group of sophomores. But she was regarding Marnie steadily, frowning slightly. Defiantly, Marnie caught her eye and stared right back.

Had Ms. Slaight talked to Mrs. Fisher? Even if she left out Marnie's gospel-inspired insult—and for some reason Marnie figured she would—she could have displayed Marnie's artistic chemistry test. More trouble . . . when all Marnie wanted, really, was to be left alone. Was that too much to ask?

Marnie broke eye contact with Mrs. Fisher. If only she could quit school altogether. But how would she live? She didn't get Skye's money for years, and Max had made it abundantly clear that she was to stay in school. Could she get a job? But doing what? Trouncing elves?

Still aware of Mrs. Fisher's gaze, Marnie pretended to be as interested as the rest of the table in what Dorothea Polley was saying about college. One of the things Marnie liked to do was to imagine that the speech coming out of the other girls' mouths was enclosed in big cartoon balloons. When anyone got too bombastic, Marnie would pull out an invisible hatpin—a long silver one with a pearl on the end, she'd decided—deftly skewer the balloon, then watch the imaginary letters flutter to the floor in glorious disarray. Pop! Pop! Pop! It was *Sesame Street* run amok, and made dinner considerably more enjoyable.

"What I want," Dorothea was now saying intensely, "what I think I need, is a really, really good drama department. And lots of opportunities to actually *act*. I mean, a college that doesn't just offer a drama *major*—*lots* of places do that—but somewhere that does a lot of *productions*. A *range* of productions. Everything from *Shake*speare to . . . to . . ." Dorothea's arm swept the air. ". . . to, oh, you know, someone very modern like . . ." The arm again; Marnie groped in the seam of her jeans for her hatpin. ". . . like . . . like . . ."

"Like Chekhov?" Jenna Lowry supplied.

Almost against her will, Marnie turned her head to glance at Jenna's expressionless face. Jenna, who was pretty, athletic, popular, and famous throughout Halsett for being gifted at literature . . . but who was not usually openly vicious.

Dorothea was bestowing a warm smile on Jenna. "Yes," she said. "That's *exactly* the kind of contemporary writer I mean."

"I thought so," murmured Jenna. Marnie watched her exchange a fast look with Tarasyn, with Barb. Dorothea, predictably, missed the byplay completely.

And suddenly Marnie was filled with a nameless

rage. So what if Dorothea didn't know Chekhov from someone Jenna "Lit/Crit" Lowry might condescend to call "modern"? So what if Dorothea was uninformed, or even an idiot? She didn't deserve to be mocked in public.

"Wait a minute," Marnie said, interrupting the conversation Jenna had just started about some new movie. Everyone turned, in surprise, toward her; Marnie rarely spoke at meals. "I thought Chekhov was a nineteenth-century playwright," she said aggressively to Jenna. "Russian, right? *The Cherry Orchard? Uncle Vanya?*"

A second passed.

Then Jenna said, blandly: "Ah, Marnie, you're thinking of *Anton* Chekhov. Dorothea and I were discussing *Jessica* Chekhov. Jessica's work is very, uh, avant-garde."

"Yes, that's right!" put in Dorothea emphatically. But she spoke a little too quickly, and you could see the alarmed white around her eyes.

Marnie ignored her. She gave Jenna a long stare. Jenna, also carefully not looking at Dorothea, lifted her chin and gave Marnie a very cool, challenging look right back.

Marnie felt her left hand clench in her lap. She had forgotten entirely about her imaginary hatpin. "I've never heard of this Jessica Chekhov. What plays has she written, Jenna? Enlighten my ignorance."

Jenna's chin had gone farther up. "Dorothea? Fill Marnie in."

"No," Marnie began. "Jenna, you're the one who—"

But Dorothea had opened her mouth. "Uh, everyone knows about Jessica Chekhov . . . Her first play was . . . was on Broadway . . . Leonardo DiCaprio was in it . . ." She stuttered on, saying one ridiculous thing after another and, throughout, staring at Marnie—not at Jenna—with helpless, increasing hatred.

Everyone sat frozen at the table. Not one person moved to stop Dorothea's babble as it increased in speed and volume and silliness—

Finally Marnie couldn't stand it. "Shut up, Dorothea," she said sharply. It worked like a slap. Dorothea drew a deep breath, looking as if any minute she would burst into a storm of tears. And in the piercing moment of complete silence that followed, all the other girls looked at Marnie as if *she* had done something awful.

Marnie tightened her hand on the imaginary hatpin until she could almost feel its bite. What she already knew was made even clearer. You were better off hanging out in cyberspace, chasing elves. Fewer people got hurt that way.

CHAPTER 3

arnie pulled the headphones off slowly, at the point at which Skye's solo harmonized with the strong soft background vocals of the chorus, before blending so perfectly into the other voices that you could no longer distinguish her individual one. Marnie had asked her mother once if she was still singing at that point, or had stopped entirely, but Skye hadn't remembered. It was all so long ago, she'd said. As far as Marnie could recall, Skye had never listened to her own vocal recordings. Of all Skye's CDs, this one was Marnie's favorite.

Or rather, had been.

She stared at the headphones in her hands. She listened to Skye's CDs all the time, and yet, more and more of late, the music—Skye herself—seemed to slip away even as Marnie listened. It became a strong, disembodied voice that had nothing to do with Marnie, that left her alone instead of sur-

18

rounding her with warmth as it used to do. The thought panicked her. Someday she might not even be able to listen anymore . . .

She closed her eyes for a second. It was just that she was tired. She was tired all the time now. She longed to sleep but knew she couldn't. Shouldn't. Not so early. She ought to do some chemistry homework. Or *any* homework, really. The only class she was on top of was precalculus, which didn't count since by some quirk she had never had to work at math.

The problem was, she really didn't want to work. If only Max would magically understand how stupid it all was, this school stuff. How pointless. Marnie knew she was right about this. If she could only leave, she would be all right . . . it was this place, not her. Those other girls—she didn't understand them, she never would. A tough school was Max's idea, since Marnie had herself insisted on boarding school. "Let's try something academically challenging," he had said, after Marnie demanded to leave the celebrity school. "You know you could be up for it if you tried." The girls' school idea had been Mrs. Shapiro's contribution, but Max had liked it, and identified Halsett within days. Marnie wondered how he'd talked them into taking her, with her—even then—erratic academic record.

Students tended to work intensely at Halsett. There was huge pressure to excel, to take advanced courses, to apply to prestigious colleges. Competition was fierce. Everybody knew everybody else's class rank. Girls cried when they got grades below

A, or when their PSAT and SAT results were less than spectacular. Some girls took drugs to be able to stay up late, work harder, harder still. A few drank to relieve the tension. Last semester, one senior had had a nervous breakdown putting together her college applications—there'd even been whispers she'd tried to slit her wrists. And right now, with college letters due to arrive in only a couple of weeks, the entire senior class looked feverish not only with fear and hope, but with a whole range of twitchier emotions as they eyed each other, added up vital statistics, and wondered: How many would Harvard take? Stanford? Yale? It was like living in a vat of boiling water.

Marnie blamed the staff, yes, and society, okay, but the other girls all appeared to be brainwashed puppets! *Cannibalistic* puppets from a horror movie, at that. Take Jenna Lowry, with her sly remarks about Chekhov. Everything else aside, it was just so, so *Halsett*. It made you sick. More specifically, Jenna made Marnie sick. The perfect Halsett girl. Marnie felt her dinnertime rage return, and was glad. It filled that empty place where Skye no longer was.

Right after dinner, Jenna had come up next to Marnie as all the girls walked back to the dorms. Marnie had stopped dead in the road and confronted her. "What?"

Jenna spat back, "You made me do it."

"Oh, please. Tell that one to your mommy." Despite the dim campus ground lighting, Marnie saw Jenna's lips tighten.

"You—you . . ."

"Me, me," mimicked Marnie.

"Exactly," said Jenna viciously.

Marnie felt a clutch at her stomach. "That's an amazing criticism coming from you. At least I don't prop up my ego by putting other people down publicly."

"Dorothea would never have known if you hadn't pushed me!"

"What power I have over you. I'm flattered."

"You—you—"

"Didn't we do that part of the conversation already?"

Jenna had stomped off, and Marnie had watched her go with some satisfaction. But it had faded fast. And now, remembering, it didn't make her feel as justified as she had thought it would.

Oh, God. Marnie opened her eyes again and stared at Skye's CD. It used to be that Marnie could simply concentrate and she'd know just what Skye might have said about any situation. Sometimes she still could. Sometimes.

Not now.

After a minute she fitted the CD carefully back into its case. Then, without thinking at all, she turned on her computer and sat down. And in a few minutes . . .

Greetings, Sorceress, said the Elf. *I thought I'd see you here tonight.*

Marnie's heart lightened. She leaned over her keyboard.

Three hours later, Marnie had the Elf backed into a twisty little passage with only one truly viable exit option, an airshaft that was—barely—climbable with artificial aid.

Or, he could go down another level of tunnels and take his chances with the Rubble-Eater. *Who hasn't eaten for a while,* Marnie told the Elf helpfully.

It hadn't been difficult, really, getting the Elf into this section of tunnel. The Elf was always willing to take chances. The challenge had been figuring out what six items he was holding—well, five items, actually, because the sixth was the magical spellbook that he'd stolen from Marnie last night. She'd had to make sure that, when the Elf reached this point, all of those five items would be more important, more necessary to his survival, than the spellbook.

He had to drop something, of course, in order to pick up the grappling hook Marnie had thoughtfully placed at the entrance to the airshaft. The Elf couldn't make it up the airshaft without the grappling hook. Marnie could, because she was a sorceress and self-levitation was among her documented powers.

She smiled at her computer screen, where the little animated green figure that represented the Elf was standing perfectly still.

Drop cloak of invisibility, said the Elf. *Get grappling hook.*

Are you sure? Marnie happily typed in the chat window. *Have you forgotten where the airshaft leads? The Mountain King doesn't like elves.*

He doesn't like sorceresses, either, snapped back the Elf.

Ah, but we have a treaty tonight.

The green Elf pulsed on the screen. Then: *Drop rubies. Get cloak of invisibility.*

Interesting move, Elf. Marnie almost laughed at the screen. *But are you sure you want to do that?* In the few seconds that followed, she imagined that, wherever in the real world the Elf was, he was swearing. Out loud.

I'm not giving up the spellbook, said the Elf eventually.

Don't be such a poor sport, Marnie typed back. *What good is it to you? Elves can't be sorcerers; it's in the guild rules. You knew it when you decided on your character. Go on, drop the spellbook.*

Another few seconds ticked by. Then:

NEVER! shouted the Elf.

Manners, manners, typed Marnie.

The Elf whipped back: *I'll shout if I want to. By the way, do you happen to have a treaty with the Rubble-Eater, too?*

Marnie stared at her screen. What . . . ?

WIELD CLOAK OF INVISIBILITY! yelled the Elf, clearly inspired. *PICK UP RUBIES! DROP GRAP-PLING HOOK! JUMP DOWN AIRSHAFT!*

The Elf disappeared from Marnie's screen.

Marnie burst out laughing. The Elf was never dull; you had to give him that. *Down* the airshaft. With her spellbook, too. And without the grappling hook.

It was too funny. The Elf must have thought that the Rubble-Eater wouldn't see him with the cloak on. But the Rubble-Eater was blind, and functioned by sound and smell. Most likely, the Elf was toast. At least for tonight. Marnie wouldn't even need to go after him herself.

She ought to study, or just go to bed, and chase the spellbook tomorrow night. But on the other hand . . .

Pick up grappling hook, she typed, and clicked Send.

On the other hand, she hadn't visited the Lair of the Rubble-Eater in a very long time.

Jump down airshaft, she typed.

"Wait for me, Elf," she murmured aloud.

CHAPTER
4

Marnie slept peacefully through the next morning's classes, arising rested and refreshed exactly when she wished to. She had to laugh when she sat up in bed and peered at the alarm clock. Sleep was an excellent thing. She stretched luxuriously. She'd had nearly nine hours of it.

Plus, she had her spellbook back. Take that, Elf!

There was absolutely no sense in rushing to make her last few classes. Since her absence would already have been noticed, she might as well get in trouble for the whole day. *Embrace the inevitable.* Skye had written that somewhere. Marnie took a long, hot shower, and then did two loads of laundry in the dorm basement. How fabulous not to have to fight several other girls for the machines! She idly watched her jeans and socks rotate in the dryer and wondered if, after all, she should devote some time during spring break to catching up. It made sense. If she could get through the next two months, there'd only be one year of high school left. She didn't have to be part of the Halsett madness; she could easily find a random noncompetitive college and major in something or other, waste time until she was twenty-one. Then she could do as she liked, whatever that was. Trounce elves around the clock.

Yes, she should do a little work now. Lie low. Endure.

Of course she'd planned to spend a lot of time online during break, but there was no reason she couldn't study also, without classes to interfere and soak up hours. In fact, it wouldn't hurt the Elf to wonder where she was, if she didn't show up in Paliopolis for a while. Marnie wondered if she'd be able to stay away for a whole week. Wouldn't sheer boredom entice her online? Well, no big deal either way. She could cope. Irrationally feeling even more cheerful, she pulled her clothes from the dryer, stuffed them into her laundry basket, and bounced upstairs to her room.

The peace of the early afternoon had ended. Marnie's corridor was filled with noise: footsteps, doors opening and shutting, the shrill of voices. Ahead, across from Marnie's room and in the open doorway of Tarasyn Pearce's, stood Tarasyn and Jenna Lowry. The girls stopped talking as Marnie approached. Marnie ignored them and fished one-handed for her room key.

After a tense moment, Tarasyn said, "Marnie, Mrs. Fisher just slipped a note under your door. She asked us where you were, but we didn't know."

Mrs. Fisher. Marnie's stomach clenched. A dorm

counselor never rests. "Well, now you do know," said Marnie, nudging her door open with her hip. She hoisted the basket just a little in her arms and added merrily: "Laundry. Bane of my life."

"But, um, Marnie—" Tarasyn began.

Jenna cut in, sweetly. "Don't step on Mrs. Fisher's note."

"Thank you, Jenna." Marnie flashed an equally sweet smile. "You're always so considerate of others." She looked down. A cream-colored "Halsett Academy for Girls" envelope sat on the dusty floor inches from Marnie's sneakers. Marnie deposited the laundry basket on the floor just inside the room and picked up the envelope. It didn't weigh much. And it wasn't hard to guess what it said. She just wished . . . well, it would have been better if this had come after spring break, when she'd have some work to show. Assuming she would. Suddenly her mind did a seesaw: maybe she wanted to be thrown out. But then Max would just make her go elsewhere. Mrs. Shapiro had once suggested Brearley, which was right in New York City. Marnie couldn't bear to live there, with Max and Mrs. Shapiro, playing family. It was hard enough summers, when Max made her come home.

She could feel Jenna and Tarasyn's dense curiosity. You'd think the envelope contained something of importance. She turned back to them. "Would you two like me to read it out loud?"

"Oh, no!" Tarasyn actually ducked her head in embarrassment. But Marnie was watching Jenna. Who said, defiantly: "Since you offer."

Marnie extended the envelope until it was only a

breath's length from Jenna's nose. "I have a better idea," she said. "You read it to me."

"Fine," spat Jenna. Rage stiffened her entire body. Marnie leaned smiling against the door frame. Jenna tore the envelope open, unfolded a single sheet of paper, and scanned it. "Tomorrow at eight A.M.," she said rapidly, "you're supposed to have a conference with Mrs. Fisher. And the dean. If you don't come they'll expel you. Satisfied? Here." She thrust the letter back toward Marnie.

"Thank you," Marnie said politely. She did not take the letter, and Jenna's expression distorted even further. Marnie stepped back into her room and closed her door, quietly, on Jenna and the letter Jenna still held.

She took in one deep breath, trying to ignore a pang of misgiving regarding Jenna. *You should only alienate folks when you mean and want to do it,* Skye had said once, thoughtfully, after getting off the phone with an oily record producer. *It should never be an accident.*

God, I hate school, Marnie thought. It was slowly turning her into someone else. Someone Skye might not even recognize. Someone who made enemies . . .

Determinedly, she thought about the conference. They must be planning to give her one last chance. If they were definitely going to throw her out, they wouldn't have threatened to do so if she didn't come to the meeting, right?

She shrugged, then straightened her shoulders. Well, okay. She knew when to stop pushing. She did.

She'd be good. *Their* version of good.

Across the room, on her computer monitor, Marnie's screensaver program drew, dissolved, and redrew an endless cycle of spinning mazes. She stared at it for a while. Then she sat down before it and logged on to Paliopolis, even though it was far too early for the Elf to be there. She tapped her fingers slowly on the keyboard for a moment and then retrieved and read his character profile. Yes, she'd remembered correctly: he had registered an e-mail address. She frowned, not quite believing she'd break her own "no outside contact" rule. But this was a special case. For the first time, she sent him a direct e-mail.

Hey, loser. I'm not going to be around for a while. I have to make sure I don't flunk out of school. See you later . . . maybe.

That night, she did homework and went to bed at eleven. And the next morning, she showed up at Mrs. Fisher's office for the conference exactly one minute before eight.

However, Mrs. Fisher was not there. And after fifteen minutes of waiting outside her locked office door, Marnie figured out that the conference must be at the dean's office, across campus. Clenching her fists, she took an extra moment to curse Jenna for having synopsized—rather than read aloud—Mrs. Fisher's note.

And then, more honestly, she cursed herself, for not taking the note back from Jenna.

Then she raced. But by the time she got to the dean's office, she was a full half hour late. A half hour during which Mrs. Fisher, the dean, and

Max—on the speakerphone in New York—had been waiting.

Waiting and discussing Marnie's March Internet access statement. Mrs. Fisher had a copy in her hand and a smug "aha!" look on her face.

CHAPTER 5

It was the definition of irony, Marnie decided that evening, bitterly. She'd gone to the meeting full of penitence; she'd even brought last night's homework as actual evidence of reform. But neither Mrs. Fisher nor the dean had been interested. They'd pushed the Internet statement in her face. Someone had taken a thick red marker and circled the total number of connected hours for the month of March. As if you wouldn't notice it otherwise. One hundred and ninety-three.

One ninety-three, rhymes with coffee and tea. And fiddle-dee-dee. Money-back guarantee.

Mrs. Fisher was watching her.

Okay. Six point two hours online per day; Marnie supposed it *was* a lot. But weren't there people who spent even more time watching television?

"Marnie, what do you have to say about this?" Mrs. Fisher's eyes were full of a kind of superior

31

pity. And seeing it, Marnie just couldn't help herself.

"Dayum," she said cheerfully. "I coulda sworn I hit two hundred. Well, maybe this month. Anybody care to bet? Closest without going over?"

There was a brief silence. Then the dean said to Mrs. Fisher, "I see what you mean."

Mrs. Fisher nodded. "This is not a joke," she said to Marnie. "You've raised passive-aggressive behavior practically to an art form, but we can see the truth behind it. We are talking about a very real addiction. Even a dangerous one." The sympathy returned to her eyes, though now it looked a little forced. "We were on the point of expelling you. But I've checked all your old Internet access statements, and this one is the worst. This is clearly a growing problem. We can help you, though."

Marnie opened her mouth to roar a spontaneous Handel-inspired *Hallelujah,* and then, barely in time, remembered that she'd come here intending to make amends. Still . . . addiction? Oh, please.

Mrs. Fisher's chest had expanded like a strutting pigeon's. "Don't you want to fit in better here? Be more like the others? You'd be happier then."

Marnie's brain skidded to a full stop. For a second she couldn't believe her ears. Fit in? *Fit in? That* would make her happier?

"Something to think about, hmm?" said the insufferable Mrs. Fisher. Marnie gritted her teeth as the woman continued. "We have a plan to help you beat this thing. First, Ms. Slaight will be coordinating tutoring sessions for you next week during break. She volunteered. You need help in everything but math. You should know, Marnie, that Ms. Slaight has been very much your friend. We had a meeting with all your teachers, and she was one of those who argued that you can succeed here, and we should give you another chance."

What? Ms. Slaight? Oh, no, Marnie thought. Anyone else, please—anyone but her. This was intolerable.

"That should help you get caught up in your classes," Mrs. Fisher continued. "And it will keep you really busy, so that you don't even have time to think about the computer. We're confident that with some concentration, you'll catch up fairly quickly. No one questions your intelligence, Marnie. Are you willing to work hard?"

Marnie looked down. She thought about pulling out her hatpin; transforming it into some kind of magic wand. She'd wave it at Mrs. Fisher and the dean and turn them into Internet-crazed fiends. The dean would find herself watching the Africam obsessively hour after hour in hopes of seeing a rhino visiting the water hole. Mrs. Fisher would bid wildly on secondhand figurines and limited-edition plates from the Franklin Mint, building a huge collection that she'd stack up, in unopened boxes, all over her apartment. Max would day-trade Internet stock until his eyeballs gleamed red. And then—

Marnie disciplined herself. She nodded.

"You'll make a serious commitment to work hard, to catch up?" Mrs. Fisher was insisting.

They wanted it out loud. Marnie said dully: "Yes. Sure. Okay."

Mrs. Fisher's lips pursed at her tone, but she

nodded anyway. "Good. Next, we are removing your computer from your room. When you need a computer for your schoolwork, you may use one in the library."

The dean added, "Under supervision, of course."

For one entire minute, Marnie could not think at all.

Then she said: "Excuse me?"

The dean said evenly, "You heard us the first time, Marnie. No computer. We know how you must feel. But you're not to be trusted, any more than an alcoholic can be trusted with a bottle."

Marnie watched the dean's lips move. She watched Mrs. Fisher nod in agreement. The words floated by her ears. She cocked her head at Mrs. Fisher. Distantly she wondered, was Max buying this? Why was he so silent?

Then she thought of the Elf. She'd actually already told him she was going to be away for a while. He wouldn't even wonder where she was. He wouldn't give her another thought. Huh. Funny how much that hurt. In a remote way, of course.

Mrs. Fisher was going on. "Lastly, when break is over, you'll begin seeing the school psychologist. Three times a week. To talk about these very serious issues; to get a grip on your dysfunctional areas."

A psychiatrist? Dysfunctional areas?

For several seconds, as if she were on the point of fainting, Marnie's vision filled entirely with white.

Words suddenly hammered in her head; her throat. Losers! Clueless, ignorant . . . losers! How dared they talk about her being happier! A lobotomy would make her happier too, had they thought of that? Not that they were truly concerned with her happiness. They didn't care who Marnie Skyedottir was, what she wanted, what she thought—

She opened her mouth to let it all loose.

As if Max somehow knew what she was about to say, from the speakerphone came his disembodied drawl. He sounded tired. "Marnie. I have something to say too. The thing is, Skye wanted you to have a good education. She said so very distinctly in her will. It was one of her charges to me and to you. It meant a lot to her. You know that. Please, can't you focus on it?"

Marnie paused. The stream of furious words in her head stuttered to a stop. They were still there, but somehow she couldn't reach them.

What would Skye want? Not for Marnie to move in lockstep with others; Marnie was sure of that. The psychiatrist? Skye had believed in self-examination, but not when it was against one's will!

And the computer . . . ah, Skye wouldn't have cared.

Mrs. Fisher, the dean, Max—they were ignorant and wrong! The problem wasn't her online time. And it wasn't fair that these people should have power over her, should be able to make these summary judgments. It would be years until she'd be free; how could she wait until then?

She tried to calm herself. She looked away from the nearly irresistible provocation of Mrs. Fisher's and the dean's face, down at her own hands. They were very different from Skye's hands—squarer palms, shorter fingers, rounder nails—and that was peculiar, wasn't it, because her feet were shaped exactly like Skye's. Marnie could remember, vividly, how Skye had laughed when Marnie'd noticed their feet. Marnie had been ten. They'd plunked down on the sofa side by side, propped up their feet on the coffee table, and just looked. Skye had said reflectively, *I like feet. They're so useful.* Wiggling her toes, Marnie had decided right then that she liked feet too—all feet, even ugly ones.

A long time ago, from that day to this. All at once Marnie was aware that she had developed a nasty headache.

"Marnie?" insisted Mrs. Fisher. Her voice was soft now, which was good. Marnie exhaled softly. Suddenly and fiercely, she needed to get out of there.

The dean was biting her lip. "Well, Marnie? We're pressed for time. Mrs. Fisher has laid it all out. These are the conditions under which you may remain at Halsett. Do you understand?"

Oh, yes. She understood, all right.

"Marnie?"

"Yes," said Marnie finally.

"And you agree?" asked the dean.

Oh. They wanted her to say it twice. Sadists. So Marnie liked Paliopolis better than Halsett Academy. What was so dysfunctional about that?

"Yes," said Marnie. She was just buying time, she decided. She'd think this all out later.

"Good," said the dean. "Then we're done. Excellent. Marnie, Mrs. Fisher will talk with you later about the details—the tutoring during break, and so on."

Mrs. Fisher laid a hand on Marnie's arm. "I think

you'll find," she whispered conspiratorially, "that one day you'll be glad we had this conversation."

Yes, and one day Marnie would sprout wings and flit from flower to flower singing operetta. She pulled back sharply so that Mrs. Fisher's hand dropped off her arm.

Later. She'd think this all out later. She heard Max say good-bye to the dean. He said something to Marnie, too, but she didn't listen. She couldn't. She heard the line disconnect. Fine. That was fine. That was best.

She walked, steadily, through a gray haze to the main quad. She went to her next class. Then she took some aspirin and went to the class after that.

She knew her computer would be gone when she got back to her room. And it was. But it still shocked her to see the emptiness of the desk. It made her feel—violated.

On top of which, she thought drearily, now she'd never find out if the Elf had answered her e-mail.

Which, she knew, was a silly, silly, *silly* thing to be the final straw that broke—

CHAPTER 6

The next day was Friday, the last day of classes before break. Lots of girls were leaving that afternoon; long before breakfast Marnie could hear the commotion as they packed. If last semester's break was any guide, she'd be the only one left on the floor after five o'clock.

For a moment she thought she might be making a mistake, staying here at a near-empty school instead of going to New York. But she'd set the pattern years before, made it very clear to Max that the apartment on Central Park West wasn't home and never could be. When she *was* there, Marnie always lived out of her suitcases rather than unpacking, and made sure Max and Mrs. Shapiro knew it.

She wondered, sometimes, if they were uncomfortable in that apartment as well. There was something about many of the rooms that said they were usually unoccupied.

"No family life. Yet another symptom of dysfunction," she told her weary image in the mirror. She looked terrible, so she drew on her dark eye makeup with a heavier hand than usual. She tried not to look at her empty desk but couldn't quite avoid it. It was very dusty. She couldn't remember the last time she'd cleaned.

She wondered where they'd put her computer. In some closet somewhere, right in this dorm? In Mrs. Fisher's apartment downstairs? With the Elf's e-mail probably sitting there on it, unread. It just killed her.

Then she blinked. She was a complete idiot. The meeting yesterday had truly messed up her head. Because of course she didn't need her own computer to check e-mail. She hadn't downloaded anything. Her mail was still floating in cyberspace. All she needed was any computer with a Net connection. She could skip right over from the school's server to the one on which she kept her private account. No problem.

Hel-*lo*, Elf.

With a library computer—no, that would be too blatant, especially now, without other students around to distract attention. But every Halsett girl had her own computer, and nearly everyone would be gone by this afternoon. There was sure to be someone who was careless about locking her room.

Marnie headed off to breakfast with a slightly accelerated pulse. She loved having a plan; and the specifics of figuring out how to get to a computer and access her e-mail made her feel almost as if she were in Paliopolis. Not to mention the pure joy of thwarting Mrs. Fisher, and Max, and, oh, all of them.

Take that, buffoons! Marnie stabbed her imaginary hatpin in the air.

The cafeteria was nearly empty—people skipping breakfast in favor of packing. Jenna Lowry, however, sat alone at one end of Marnie's usual table. She was reading a paperback book that she held open on the table with one hand. Half a bagel sat untouched on her tray.

Marnie knew she could plunk herself down anywhere; there were no seating arrangements for breakfast. But something in her was stubborn. She placed her tray directly across from Jenna, who scowled. Marnie lifted her orange juice glass in a mocking little salute. Jenna's nostrils flared with disdain before she returned, theatrically, to her book.

Silence.

Marnie ate and pretended to be deep in reviewing history notes. She ate more than she wanted, actually, because she sensed Jenna stealing quick looks at her and she wanted to appear unconcerned. The words on the notebook pages were a dull, meaningless jumble. She turned a page at random. Her mind wandered.

Jenna's dorm room was on the floor below Marnie's, the ground floor. Marnie found herself wondering how different the room locks could possibly be from each other. In movies and books, people were always sliding in bobby pins or credit cards and jimmying doors open. How hard could it be? She could practice on her own door first. Maybe there were even instructions up on the Net somewhere for easing locks open. She could look on . . . oh, no, she couldn't.

For a moment the horror of it all swept over her again.

Still, the idea of somehow getting to Jenna's computer wouldn't go away. Marnie found herself glancing over at her—and saw Jenna staring back, eyes narrowed.

"What are you looking at?" Jenna's palm flattened on her book.

There was something defensive about the gesture. Marnie fixed her raccoon eyes on the paperback beneath Jenna's hand. Little Miss Lit/Crit usually toted around thick classics: Dostoyevsky, Wharton, Flaubert. But this book was slender. Without thinking, Marnie blurted, "What are you reading?"

To Marnie's astonishment, Jenna blushed. It was not a faint tinge of pink that touched her face, but a full-bodied red that spread slowly and inexorably upward from her neck all the way to her hairline.

Deep inside Marnie, unexpectedly, amusement and a kind of warmth bubbled up. For a moment she forgot everything else and said, "That good, huh? Can I borrow it when you're done?"

Jenna snapped the book shut and whisked it away beneath the table. "No!" she said. To her clear horror, a little spit came flying out with the word. She jumped up from the table. "I really hate your guts," she said rapidly to Marnie. "You think you're so superior, but you make me sick, do you know that? Sick!"

Superior? All at once Marnie was enraged too.

She was just trying to get by! "Get a life, Jenna. You're obviously not satisfied with the one you have, or you wouldn't be obsessing about what you think about me, and what *I* think about me." She narrowed her eyes and took aim, knowing with infallible instinct what would hurt this particular girl terribly: "And you wouldn't be reading trashy books. Don't tell me. Harlequin romance?" She knew instantly she'd hit her target. Dead center.

Jenna hissed like a snake. "Don't you dare criticize my reading habits, you—"

"Oh, please. Spare me."

"I have a life! I have friends, which is more than you do! I even have a boyfriend, and this weekend we're going to—" Jenna stopped talking so abruptly she bit her own lip.

"Go on," Marnie said after a second. "Things were just getting interesting. I see that you *were* reading for academic purposes, then. Sort of. Although I'm not sure what kind of technique a Harlequin romance will—"

Jenna grabbed her uneaten bagel and hurled it at Marnie. Marnie dodged slightly left and the bagel went sailing over her right shoulder, bounced off the far wall with a muffled thud, and landed on the floor. A couple of kids turned and looked, but most didn't notice.

Jenna stormed out.

Marnie got up, retrieved the bagel from the floor, and threw it out. Then she bussed Jenna's abandoned tray and sat down again. She was surprised to find she was shaking.

You should only alienate folks when you mean and want to do it.

When had she, Marnie Skyedottir, become a person who meant and wanted to? How? It wasn't like her. Was it?

Marnie wrapped her arms around herself. She needed a computer, she just *needed* one. When she was online, she didn't have to think about herself.

Oh, Skye, she thought. Where are you? But she knew the answer. Memories, recordings, books . . . all the quotes in the world . . . they were not Skye.

It didn't matter. It didn't matter.

CHAPTER 7

There was a single message, a short one, waiting in Marnie's e-mail box.

It was from the Elf.

Marnie's heart leapt. Other worries faded from her mind as she stared at the one-line listing as if it were a beautifully wrapped present.

The Elf had a very interesting address, she reflected. FRD@stjoans.edu. St. Joan's was a prep school near Boston. So the Elf didn't live far away, relatively speaking.

FRD. *Fred?* No, that couldn't be the Elf's name. The Elf's name had to be something like—well, Marnie didn't know. It was impossible to think of him as anything but the Elf.

It didn't matter what his name was. Nearby or not, she was not going to meet the Elf in real life. It would spoil everything. In fact, it was almost too much to be exchanging e-mail.

Instead of opening the message, Marnie looked around Jenna's room. When a quick inspection from outside had ascertained that Jenna had left her window unlocked, Marnie had been unable to resist. Now, inside, she sat at Jenna's desk. It was dark—she didn't dare turn on a light—but she was well accustomed to seeing only in the glow from the monitor.

She could see, for instance, that Jenna was sort of a slob. Two pairs of jeans were lying on the floor near the unmade bed. A couple dozen paperback romance novels were stacked near them. And dust lay everywhere, except on a nicely framed photograph of a teenage boy in a hockey uniform. Jenna's famous boyfriend, Marnie supposed. She studied the picture, which Jenna had placed next to the computer monitor. She wondered, were this boy and Jenna right now—no, stop. Marnie *really* didn't want to imagine that scenario.

She returned her attention to Jenna's computer screen. She opened the Elf's message, and immediately all thought of Jenna vanished from her mind.

You can't be flunking out? What's the problem? It looks like I'm going to be allowed to graduate next month—can I help? I've tutored before and we can do it all online. My prices are reasonable. Your spellbook would do.

There was no signature.

A senior, Marnie thought. He's a senior at St. Joan's. She didn't know why she felt so triumphant at having the little nugget of information—almost the way she'd felt at recovering the spellbook in Paliopolis. She clicked Reply and typed, *Yes, I'm in*

45

serious danger of flunking. They have tutors lined up for me already. I'll be stuck here studying this weekend and all next week during break. Don't worry, though—I'm not dumb, just bored. Do you like St. Joan's? I'm a junior at Halsett.

She paused, tapping her fingertips lightly on the keys. She wanted . . . she had the impulse to write more, lots more. Details. But she knew it wasn't wise. The Elf wasn't a friend; she had to remember that. This was quite enough communication.

On a whim, however, she signed the e-mail: *Marnie.* It would encourage the Elf to tell her his real name. Which she sincerely hoped was not Fred.

She clicked Send. She stared at her lonely little inbox, with its single message now flagged "read." She thought about deleting it but didn't. She thought about entering the Elf's address into her empty address book but didn't do that either. She wondered when the Elf would reply. By tomorrow, surely? Could she sneak back in here in the morning? She wouldn't have to clamber dangerously through the window again; she'd simply leave the door unlocked.

At that moment a reply arrived. The Elf was online right now!

Hey, there you are. Halsett, eh? I know where that is. Yeah, St. Joan's is okay. I'll be glad to move on, though. What subjects are you having problems with?

Marnie found she was embarrassed. She simply couldn't list all of them. What if the Elf thought she was stupid? Carefully, she typed, *Chem's the worst. Paliopolis was occupying too much of my time, that's all.*

46

A reply came almost instantly. *Are you really giving the game up?*

For now, anyway, Marnie answered.

The Elf's reply was so long in coming that Marnie began to think he had rudely logged off without saying good-bye. But then it did come.

I just checked the Halsett server. Couldn't resist. Do those idiots know how insecure it is? I got right into their records. There's a back door off the Web site that any minimally competent hacker could find. Listen—there's only one Marnie listed, and I couldn't help noticing your last name. Cool. I've read a couple of your mother's books. She was a pretty interesting thinker, although I'd disagree with her concept of personal revelation. Anyway, you've got an A in Algebra II, Ms. Sorceress, but you're flunking everything else. I really can help. No charge. Well, maybe some Paliopolis pointers.

Marnie felt as if she'd been kicked in the stomach. *I couldn't help noticing your last name.* She couldn't answer. She stared at the message and she couldn't answer. And after five minutes another message arrived. For a moment she thought she couldn't open it, but then she did. It said only: *Hey, are you there?*

She couldn't answer that, either.

Then, after another five minutes, another message came. *Okay, you probably just had to go. I'm going to bed—Paliopolis is no fun without you. E me back when you can. And find some way to tell Halsett to make their g-d server secure. Take a look. All student records are completely accessible.*

That was great, Marnie thought wearily. That was

47

just great. Halsett incompetence. Well, too bad for them. She wasn't going to help them one little bit.

Moving slowly, as if she were pushing through water, she used the mouse to disconnect and then turned off Jenna's computer. Even without the glow from the monitor, the room wasn't completely dark; a little light filtered in through the windows from the streetlamps outside the dorm.

I couldn't help noticing your last name.

Thank you, Sherlock Holmes. How dare he? How dare he pry around like that? People had no right to go mucking around in other people's business. And she'd given him—*given* him!—her first name, not her last. And he hadn't even bothered to sign his own message. . . .

Marnie came abruptly to the realization that she was no longer sitting at Jenna's desk. She'd jumped up and begun pacing back and forth, had even absently kicked one of Jenna's pairs of jeans under the bed as she moved. She sighed and fished it back out with one foot, pushing it to approximately its previous location on the floor. She thought vaguely about grabbing one of Jenna's romance novels and reading it. She could use another form of escape. She sank down on the bed.

Marnie, of all people, had no right to criticize the Elf for breaking in anywhere. Look where she was sitting. Still . . .

Exhaustion crashed down on her like a wave. Her eyelids felt weighted; her limbs strengthless. She was tempted to collapse right here on top of Jenna's bed. She didn't feel like going back to her own room. Maybe for just an hour or two . . .

No. If she was smart, she'd leave now, and she'd firmly lock both the window *and* the door behind her. She'd go upstairs to her own room and sleep as blamelessly as a baby. She'd do her work tomorrow, and the day after, and all next week, and never, never, never e-mail the Elf again.

I couldn't help noticing your last name.

Suddenly it didn't seem so awful for the Elf to know. It was who she was, after all.

Behind her lids, all at once, Marnie could see Skye's face. She held her breath. At one time, it had been common in her life to feel Skye near. But not these days.

Yet now Marnie could almost hear her voice, low and sweet, as she softly sang a lullaby. And then added, still softly: *I've never understood how children can sleep after hearing that one. Pretty music, though. Don't worry about the lyrics, sweet pea. I'm here to catch you.*

A lie, Marnie thought as she drifted. A lie . . . oh, but a good lie . . .

CHAPTER 8

Marnie awoke just before dawn in a great sweat of inchoate fear. She put her hand to her chest and literally felt her heart jump against her palm. She'd been dreaming . . . the Elf, faceless (but she'd known it was him), holding Jenna in a romantic clinch from the cover of a paperback romance . . . A cyber-construct hawk, red-eyed, soaring dangerously through the alleys of Paliopolis . . . Ms. Slaight waving a book on the chemistry of DNA, shouting at Marnie, *Skyedottir, Skyedottir!* . . . Weird, mixed-up stuff.

Marnie took a deep breath, and then another, and felt herself begin to calm. She swung her legs over the side of Jenna's bed and put her head down between her knees.

Sleeping here! Why had she done that? She knew better.

This was how she'd felt after Skye died. Those

awful months living with Max and Mrs. Shapiro in New York. Max had been afraid, too; Marnie had known that instinctively. She had only been eleven then. Boarding school had been the only possible answer. It had been Marnie's idea and she'd refused to change it. Max wasn't her father, after all. She had actually asked him. Stupid, yes—she knew that now.

"No," Max had said. He'd added, hesitatingly, "I wish I were," and had begun saying something else. But somehow it had all been too much, and Marnie had run out of the room. He had tried to talk about it once, no, twice since then, but Marnie had not allowed it.

Very likely Skye had had her from a sperm bank. It was the kind of choice the author of *Spiritual and Emotional Self-Determination* would have made.

The Elf probably had a regular set of parents, down there in Boston. Maybe siblings, too. A little sister in middle school who he had to share the computer with. Here was a funny thing: Marnie couldn't imagine what the Elf looked like, but she could see the little sister clearly. She was thin, with sticklike legs, and had long straggly dirty-blond hair and glasses and a big crush on one of her older brother's friends. Her name was . . . Hannah. The Elf really loved her. Sometimes he let her hang out when his friends were over. He helped her with her homework, too, but she didn't need much help, because she was a smart little girl, Hannah. All A's. They were a smart family. Both parents taught at Harvard. No. The mother taught at M.I.T. Something technical. The father taught Spanish. The

51

whole family spent summers in Madrid. No. Barcelona. No; the father taught classics, and they summered on archeological digs all over the Mediterranean. One time the Elf actually dug up, um, something important. Actually it was Hannah who found it. . . .

Marnie drifted off into an elongated daydream that was part *The Swiss Family Robinson* and part *Raiders of the Lost Ark*. It was only the realization that the room had become considerably brighter that roused her again. What *was* her problem? She had to get back upstairs. But she paused anyway, to log back on and write the Elf a message.

Yes, I'm Skye's daughter. I think I agree with you about personal revelation being bogus, but she really and honestly believed in it.

What subjects can you help me with? At this point I just want to pass some tests. Chem, European history. Oh, and I have a couple of English papers to write. I don't suppose you have any you'd be interested in selling?

Marnie almost clicked Send, but then went back and added a smiley face icon at the end, so the Elf wouldn't think she was serious.

She got upstairs and safely inside her own bleak, computerless room without incident.

"You see how much is possible when you focus?" said Ms. Slaight just after noon on Monday.

"Yeah," said Marnie uneasily.

With Ms. Slaight standing guard, Marnie had spent the entire morning in the teacher's empty classroom, toiling through three chapters of chemistry and taking the quizzes at the end of each one. Somehow she'd managed to ignore Ms. Slaight, who, Marnie thought, was being as careful of Marnie as Marnie was of her. Once Marnie had caught Ms. Slaight watching her, but then both of them had quickly looked away. Marnie didn't want any trouble. Maybe Ms. Slaight didn't either.

Still, the woman made her itchy.

Marnie had passed all the quizzes. But her head was now overstuffed with atomic structures, molecular weights, and balanced equations, and she knew she wouldn't retain the information for long. "I want to review tonight and take the section test tomorrow," she said, and Ms. Slaight nodded.

Why not see if she could make this awful woman crack a smile? "On to history!" Marnie declared, pumping one fist in the air. But Ms. Slaight only compressed her lips.

Really, Marnie thought. Why had she volunteered to help her? Were they paying her more to do so? Maybe she'd use the bonus to buy some new clothes.

In point of fact Marnie was not due to visit her history teacher until one o'clock. That left time for lunch—or, if she was careful, a quick check-in at Jenna's room to see if the Elf had replied.

She sprinted.

He had. Sort of. He'd sent an address for a college Web site that featured an outline of important dates in European history, along with several lengthy student bulletin-board discussions. But there was no note; just the URL. Had Marnie offended him with her question about English papers?

Carefully, she wrote back, *Thanks for the URL. Looks good. I'm off now to write my first English paper, on* Wuthering Heights, *which I hated.* She hesitated, then added, *Stupid Cathy,* so he would know she'd read the book. Then she closed. *Talk to you later, I hope. Can you be online at midnight?*

Marnie sent the message and lingered, checking incoming mail several times, in hopes there'd be a quick reply. But there wasn't.

CHAPTER 9

There was also no message waiting from the Elf when Marnie checked back at eleven P.M. But he was sure to be online at midnight, as she'd asked. Wasn't he? She wrote a little note reminding him, and read it over once, twice, a third time. Then she sighed and deleted it. She'd already asked him to be there. Nothing was more pathetic than multiple messages saying the same thing. Wait—could she maybe send a note about something else, and then add the part about being online at midnight very, very casually, at the end? That would be fine . . . except she could think of nothing else to say. And anyway, it was only an hour away. She thought of checking in on Paliopolis, of looking for him there, but somehow Paliopolis had lost its savor. She kept seeing Mrs. Fisher's smug face. *Addiction.* She'd show them. She fingered her imaginary hatpin.

The Elf *had* to be on tonight. Was he truly mad at her, or was she making that up? Why had she made that crack about him selling papers? She was so utterly *stupid*. Skye would be disgusted. *Spontaneity is fine,* she'd say. *But there are things you shouldn't do without thinking first.*

Marnie *did* think first—it was just that she always seemed to be thinking the wrong things.

But *Self-pity is worse than useless,* Skye had written in one of her books. *Long-term, it's damaging.*

Marnie sighed again and felt her eyes slip shut. Rest. She needed rest. . . .

A sudden scraping noise—a key turning in a lock. Marnie froze. Behind her, the door opened. She didn't turn, couldn't turn. She heard an indrawn breath, almost a gasp. And then Jenna's voice, raspy and harsh.

"What are you doing here? This is my room!"

It was as if the very air had stilled. Marnie felt almost preternaturally aware. She could feel Jenna behind her, in the doorway. She could smell her smoky rage. In the space of a second, behind her closed eyelids, Marnie looked down a long corridor of future possibilities and saw them all leading to the same place: expulsion. Once Jenna reported her, this transgression, added to her academic problems, would put a finish to her career at Halsett. She didn't know why she had ever thought leaving might be a good thing. It wouldn't be. She knew now: it would be no different anywhere else. *She* would be no different anywhere else.

She was just . . . trapped.

Jenna slammed the door. It broke the spell, and

56

Marnie got up and faced her. Jenna was breathing like a bull. But her face was blotchy, her eyes puffy, and—and—

The words popped out of Marnie's mouth without volition. "What's happened? Are you okay? My God, Jenna, what's *wrong*?"

Jenna's whole body was shaking, as if the floor were being jackhammered. Marnie had never seen anything like it. She crossed the room in two strides and grabbed Jenna's arms.

"You're hyperventilating," Marnie said. "Sit." She forced Jenna to sit on the floor—it took surprisingly little effort—and to put her head down between her knees. "Close your eyes," Marnie said. "Empty your mind. One deep breath. Hold it. Now let it out slowly. And now—again. Shhh. Slow. Again." She could hear Skye's soothing tones in her own voice. She kept her hand on Jenna's back, feeling her breathing, feeling the shaking, rubbing a little, alarmed. Should she run and pound on Mrs. Fisher's door? But she couldn't leave Jenna, not like this. She felt as if she needed to physically keep Jenna from falling apart.

Jenna was crying, messily, snuffily.

Marnie's mind whirred. That hockey boy. This must be about him. "It's okay," she murmured, over and over, not because she believed it, but because it was the kind of thing one said. She wondered exactly what had happened.

After a while, Jenna's shaking slowed to a fine trembling. At least she was definitely getting air in, Marnie thought, her own anxiety lessening.

Jenna kept her head down.

"It's okay," Marnie said again. And again.

Eventually Jenna replied. "No. Not okay." Her breath caught and Marnie returned to rubbing her back. Vaguely she was aware that this was wildly ironic, her trying to comfort Jenna Lowry. But she was the only one here.

Her right leg went to sleep under her, and then turned completely numb, and occasionally she looked up from the floor and bleakly watched Jenna's screensaver speed through an endless tunnel of stars. Beneath it, she knew, was her own online session, still engaged. Twelve o'clock had come and gone, and even if the Elf had logged on and sent an e-mail message, Marnie would not be able to respond. Meanwhile, Jenna cried as if she needed to flood the world.

Finally she stopped. She jerked her body forward away from Marnie's hand and, her face concealed, said huskily but very clearly: "Get out."

Marnie was both relieved and alarmed. "Jenna, are you sure—"

"Get out!"

"All right," Marnie said. Somehow, on her numb leg, she managed to stand. Jenna didn't raise her head, and Marnie cast one look at the computer. All her messages were sitting there; a mere click would open any of them. She wanted desperately to at least reboot the computer, break the connection. Part of her mind screamed at her to do it, that Jenna was in no condition to intervene.

"Get out!" If Jenna's throat hadn't been raw, the words would have been a scream.

Marnie left and closed the door behind her. Through it, however, she could hear Jenna's gasps, renewed, though not as dreadful as before. She stood uncertainly in the corridor, wondering again about getting Mrs. Fisher. But if she were Jenna—if this *were* about the hockey boy—she'd want to be alone.

Marnie stood in the corridor for quite a long time. Eventually she sank down on the floor, her back against the painted concrete block wall, and closed her eyes against the harsh glare of the corridor lightbulbs. She spent the rest of the night like that, counting her life's mistakes like little black sheep and wondering drearily why she felt she had to be there . . . just in case Jenna needed someone.

"Marnie? Marnie, wake up! What are you doing here? Marnie!"

Marnie's eyelids did not seem able to come unstuck. She could feel someone shaking her shoulder. She knew exactly where she was: in a cold little heap on the linoleum floor outside Jenna's room. And she knew why. She swallowed a groan and managed to open one eye. Mrs. Fisher was kneeling, leaning over Marnie, her forehead furrowed.

"Why, hello there," Marnie croaked. She put one hand up—her whole arm was stiff—and managed to rub her other eye open. Ow. "Mrs. Fisher. Good morning."

The door of Jenna's room opened. Jenna stood there, looking more or less ordinary in a robe.

Marnie gaped at her, and then at Mrs. Fisher. She sat up and tried to get her brain in gear. Mrs. Fisher was looking from one girl to the other, frowning.

"Jenna?" Mrs. Fisher said. "I thought you'd gone home for break. Is something wrong?"

"No, no," said Jenna quickly. "I just—um, some of my little cousins were over and I realized it was impossible to get any work done at home, so I just stayed for the weekend. I, um, I had my mother drop me off last night. I'm sorry, I should have called you first. . . ."

Jenna's parents thought she was staying here at school throughout break, Marnie realized with a sudden flash of insight. While Jenna skipped off with hockey boy . . .

Mrs. Fisher was frowning at Jenna.

"Me," said Marnie brightly, "I just fell asleep out here. Wow, how embarrassing. And how awful for you, Mrs. Fisher. Coming across me like that. I'm really embarrassed. Well, I guess I've figured out why they invented the bed." She staggered to her feet. "Have you ever slept on linoleum? It's hard, you know? And cold. In fact, what I really think I should do is go and take a hot shower. So if you'll both just excuse me—"

"Marnie." Mrs. Fisher stood in the way of escape.

"Oh," said Marnie. "I suppose you're wondering what I was doing here. Well. It's very simple. Very simple. I saw Jenna coming in last night, and this morning I had a question I wanted to ask her, but she wasn't up yet. Uh, this was *early* this morning. So I just sat down to wait and well, the rest you know."

"Really," said Mrs. Fisher skeptically.

Marnie stood her ground. "Yes, I just fell asleep. I must have been more tired than I realized." She couldn't resist adding: "I've been working hard, you know. I passed several chemistry quizzes yesterday."

Mrs. Fisher's lips compressed. She studied the two girls. "Jenna is up now," she said to Marnie. "Go ahead and ask her your question."

Marnie turned to Jenna. When you looked carefully, from straight on, you could see the night's tears. "No," Marnie said clearly, drawing Mrs. Fisher's attention back to her. "I'm sorry. I can't ask Jenna my question in front of you. It's private."

Mrs. Fisher's whole being radiated disbelief and suspicion. But she said only: "You and I will talk about this later. Go get that shower now." She turned to Jenna. Marnie ran upstairs and into her room. Perforce, Jenna would have to take care of herself now.

Marnie's phone rang five minutes later. It was Jenna. "I don't know what you think you're up to," she said, "but I want to be very clear about something. Keep away from me. I don't need your help."

Marnie listened to Jenna's breathing. "Okay," she said finally, but by then she was speaking to no one. Jenna had hung up.

After a minute, Marnie did too.

CHAPTER 10

"Ready for the section test?" said Ms. Slaight the instant Marnie came into the chemistry classroom.

"I still want to give it a try, but . . ." Marnie trailed off in the middle of her prepared excuses and frankly stared. Ms. Slaight was dressed with unusual formality, in a red suit with a long jacket. The outfit screamed its newness. And Ms. Slaight had a new expression on her face, too—sort of excited and also, Marnie thought, maybe a little frightened. Marnie had never seen her wearing makeup before. Her thickly applied lipstick actually glittered.

Marnie had been staring too long; she had to say something. Lots of people dressed up for work, right? So what if Ms. Slaight never had before? And so what if it was only Marnie here today? "Er, you look very nice, Ms. Slaight."

62

"Thank you," Ms. Slaight said, smiling directly at Marnie.

Maybe Ms. Slaight had a date later—though somehow Marnie couldn't quite imagine it—and she'd not only dressed up for it, but it had put her in an excellent mood.

Marnie couldn't help herself. "Are you going somewhere special, Ms. Slaight?"

"Well, Marnie." The lipsticked lips smiled yet again, looking even more surreal. "You worked so hard yesterday that I thought you deserved a treat. So, after the test, I'd like to take you out for lunch. To the Halsett Grille." And as Marnie gaped in astonishment, Ms. Slaight finished awkwardly, "I'm aware we got off on the wrong foot. I'd like us to start again."

Marnie was reeling. Lunch? Out? With Ms. Slaight? Had she stepped through the looking glass?

Ms. Slaight added, all in a rush, "I've never been to the Halsett Grille—I just haven't had the opportunity before, but I understand it's very nice."

"Yes, it is," Marnie managed weakly. "I've been there with my guardian."

"Well?" said Ms. Slaight. "Will you come with me?"

Marnie looked at her teacher's transparently hopeful face and was consumed by curiosity. Here was Ms. Slaight, turning the other cheek with a vengeance. Why? Plus, that new outfit, and her open desire to go to the stupid Halsett Grille, where they put out three forks when you ordered a glorified grilled cheese . . . In short, Marnie couldn't help feeling just the tiniest bit sorry for Ms. Slaight. Didn't she have anyone else in her life to go to lunch with?

"Yes," said Marnie. "Thank you. I'd be very pleased."

Ms. Slaight positively beamed. "Wonderful. I felt sure we could be friends if we just got past our misunderstandings. We can agree to let bygones be bygones. Right?"

"Sure," said Marnie uncertainly. Polite, maybe. But friends?

"We'll leave right after you take this test, then. Um . . . after you change, of course."

Marnie clenched her teeth for just a second. She knew perfectly well that, despite the restaurant's haughtiness, the people having lunch at the Halsett Grille would be wearing casual, preppy clothes. Ms. Slaight's suit would fit in no better than Marnie's own loud attire. Oh, well, why not make the teacher happy? Marnie knew there was a short black dress stashed somewhere in her closet. "Okay," she said grimly. "I'll change."

Ms. Slaight nodded as if there'd been no other possible outcome. Utterly bemused, Marnie sat down to take—to *try* to take—the chemistry test.

The world is a strange place, full of strange people, including us. Another of Skye's aphorisms, and Marnie supposed it, too, was true.

"Order anything you like," said Ms. Slaight expansively. Her good mood, Marnie figured, would dissolve after lunch when she corrected Marnie's

64

test. Marnie had worked hard on Monday, but she didn't fool herself. If she passed, it would be a near thing. Jenna's fault. The test material had been in Marnie's head yesterday, before she slept in the corridor.

No. Not Jenna's fault. Her own.

And what would the Elf be thinking about Marnie's no-show last night? She *had* to find another way to get her e-mail. . . .

Ms. Slaight ordered filet mignon.

"And you, miss?" said the waiter, turning too quickly to Marnie. Ms. Slaight had to clear her throat to get his attention back so she could order a salad. Marnie winced. She had seen the waiter's eyes flick disparagingly over Ms. Slaight's cheap, too-dressy suit. It made her angry, perhaps most of all because she was harboring the same thoughts.

Her imp seized her. She could control which of them he gossiped about in the kitchen!

"I'd just like a plate of mashed potatoes, please," said Marnie, with grand disregard for the contents of the menu. "With a lot of butter. Oh, and I won't need these." Retaining only her fork, she handed the rest of the cutlery over.

"Yes, miss," said the waiter, and left. Marnie looked up at Ms. Slaight and realized, too late, that she was shocked. Had misunderstood, and thought Marnie was insulting *her*.

There was no way to explain without making the situation worse.

The silence lasted a full two minutes. Then Ms. Slaight appeared to gather herself. She swallowed once or twice; Marnie saw the movement of her throat. And then she said, "Marnie. I wanted to ask you some things about . . . about Skye."

Something inside Marnie snapped.

Afterward she couldn't remember exactly what she had said. That she had made some kind of a scene, she knew. That she had yelled, she knew. Some of the words floated through her head. And by the time Marnie finished, she was trembling, not unlike the way Jenna had the night before.

How dare you think you can buy my confidence with a lunch! Do you think I'm stupid? Or were you imagining you could buy stories about Skye with a passing grade? So you could sell them to some tabloid? Was that what you were thinking? Well, you're not fit to even say her name! You're nobody! Do you hear me? You're nobody!

Ms. Slaight sat across the table, her eyes glistening, her body rigid.

Finally Marnie stopped yelling. The fog around her began to clear. Vaguely she became aware of other people in the restaurant, listening.

Ms. Slaight got up. She was not without dignity. She walked out, only tripping once, slightly, on her unaccustomed heels.

Suddenly, fully conscious of all the stares, Marnie held her head high. She summoned the waiter and paid the check for the meal that hadn't been delivered. When she'd figured in the tip, she had exactly ninety cents left to her name.

It was ten miles back to campus. Well, Marnie would have a lot to think about while walking. Like

66

her newly inevitable expulsion. And . . . and other things.

When had her life become such a mess? How?

She had a terrible headache and a dark, dark feeling of impending doom. She hadn't a clue what Skye would have done in this situation. She wasn't sure Skye—even Skye, so famous for airing her emotions, her opinions—would have let loose in the restaurant.

You should only alienate folks when you mean and want to do it.

Well, that was fine. A fine philosophy. For those who could control themselves. For those who weren't on the edge . . .

How had she got here?

Marnie left the restaurant. To her surprise, Ms. Slaight's battered Volkswagen Jetta was pulled up to the curb just outside the door. Ms. Slaight sat upright in the driver's seat, her window rolled down and both her hands flat on the wheel.

"I am a teacher," she said evenly. "You are a student in my charge. I am responsible for getting you back to campus. Get in."

"I'll walk," said Marnie.

Ms. Slaight turned her head and looked fully at Marnie. "You will get in now."

Marnie got in. Ms. Slaight started the motor. Marnie closed her eyes, feeling the tension in the car like a physical force. Miles passed, and then Ms. Slaight stopped the car. "Get out," she said.

Marnie opened her eyes. Everybody was telling her to get out, these days. They were not on campus. Where were they? "You want me to walk the rest—"

"Get out," said Ms. Slaight.

There was something in her voice. Worse than before. Worse than ever before.

My fault, Marnie thought. My fault.

Marnie got out. She would rather walk anyway.

But Ms. Slaight got out too. She grasped Marnie's arm and forced her away from the car. She looked down into Marnie's face, and her expression was like nothing Marnie had ever seen before. It hypnotized her. As if from a distance, she could hear Ms. Slaight speaking.

"I didn't want it to be this way between us, Marnie Skyedottir. But from the very first time I met you, I think I knew that it would have to be." And she raised her other hand. There was something in her clenched fist.

Marnie later remembered everything else, but not the actual feel of the sharp blow to her head.

CHAPTER
11

Waking up again—a few hours later? the next morning? afternoon?—was among the worst experiences of Marnie's life. Not absolutely the worst; nothing could top the weeks after the plane crash that killed Skye. Marnie had retched helplessly nearly every morning then, too.

Just not over a concrete floor.

And her head had not hurt quite so much, perhaps.

And beneath her, her bed—oh, God. Marnie rolled quickly to her side again and retched a little more. She hadn't had lunch, so there wasn't much to come up. She kept her eyes closed and rested her forehead on the back of her hand. Canvas was stretched on the cot frame beneath her, silence hung heavy around her, and dull artificial light burned beyond her closed eyelids.

She remembered everything. Which did not help.

Drearily, breathing carefully in and out, in and out, she reflected that she'd do anything for a glass of flat ginger ale. Well, she wasn't psychic, but she had the feeling she was not going to get it. She felt her lips curve into an involuntary grim smile and then rapidly retreat to a compressed line.

She reached up and gingerly explored her left temple with her fingers. There was a large bandage taped there. That was something; some care had been taken. She felt its edges; then a soft center of cotton. Beneath— She inhaled in a rapid little pant, and then took her hand down and tried to regulate her breathing again. She longed to curl up into a tight ball but was afraid to move. It wasn't just her head. Her whole body ached, as if she'd been thrown down a flight of stairs.

She opened her eyes and looked blearily out at the room. It was a small square, with cement-block walls, no windows, and the dank feeling of a basement. The only objects in the room seemed to be the folding cot on which Marnie was lying, and a child's large plastic sand bucket that incongruously depicted Yertle the Turtle. A single bare lightbulb hung suspended from the high ceiling, at least twelve feet up. A wooden door—the only exit—sat in the middle of the opposite wall; the lack of visible hinges indicated that it opened outward.

In movies, Marnie reflected sourly, doors always opened inward, so that imprisoned people could hide behind them and attack whoever took a few steps into the room. Of course, in movies imprisoned people didn't lie as if paralyzed, afraid to cause more pain by moving, longing for ginger ale.

Lack of a toilet never seemed to trouble them. They jumped briskly up despite any number of injuries and conceived clever plans.

Marnie was not capable of a clever plan at this moment, but cautiously, as if this too would hurt, she began trying to think.

Initially, after Skye died, Max had been very concerned about possible kidnappers. He'd conducted careful interviews about security at the first school Marnie attended, gotten references from the rich parents of current and previous students, and even consulted with Skye's old bodyguard firm. Security was vital, he had said.

But over time, the danger of kidnappers had somehow slipped down on the list of things to consider—if not entirely out of the picture. Marnie herself had not given it a thought in years. There'd been no reason; nothing to trigger any alarm.

Ms. Slaight. Who'd have guessed it? Did she have coconspirators? Was this truly a kidnapping, or just some comedy of errors? Maybe Ms. Slaight had lost her mind temporarily. Given the whole sequence of events, this seemed most likely to Marnie. Everyone at the Halsett Grille had seen them together.

Nothing about this felt like the professional kidnapping operations that had been described to her so thoroughly. She wasn't in handcuffs or blindfolded or even tied up.

Marnie was suddenly possessed by the desire to laugh hysterically. Simultaneously, her stomach contracted again, and she rolled instinctively into a ball, even though her head hurt more from the movement, as she'd known it would. She panted a little, and after a minute or two the pain retreated again to an intense background throb. Then, slowly, she became aware of feeling cold.

She unlocked her knees and tilted her chin down to look in the direction of her feet. There was a folded blanket at the end of the cot. She snagged it with one foot and dragged it upward. She huddled beneath it and began to feel warmer. That was another mistake she'd made, getting into this dress instead of staying in her jeans and wool sweater. Not that she was counting mistakes.

She wondered what was happening back at Halsett Academy. Had she been missed? It wasn't like anybody would care that she wasn't there. Jenna Lowry, for one, would rejoice.

To think Marnie had actually believed she had a problem when she couldn't find a computer to e-mail the Elf. What an idiot she was.

She retched again over the side of the cot, though this time nothing actually came out. Looking distastefully away from the area, she spotted something out of the corner of her eye, on the floor near the head of the cot. Was it a bottle? A plastic bottle?

By dint of heroic effort, Marnie reached out and grabbed her prize. Not ginger ale, but President's Choice lemon-lime seltzer. It was ridiculous how weak she was; the bottle felt as if it weighed twenty pounds. Somehow she heaved it up onto the cot with her. For a minute, it was enough just to hold it. Then she began to think about having a drink.

The best way to do that would be to sit upright. Marnie's throbbing head told her she had exerted herself all she could right now. But her mouth and throat were desperate. She managed to prop herself up against the wall. There was one awful moment when her fingers couldn't grip the twist-top sufficiently well to break the seal and open the bottle. Somehow she succeeded. She drank quite a lot, then firmly re-capped the bottle. But then she was attacked by a wave of dizziness. She dropped the bottle and heard it roll away. She closed her eyes. She thought again, still distantly, about the lack of a toilet. The Yertle the Turtle bucket?

Please, no.

Maybe this was worse, in some ways, than after Skye died.

Somebody else—the Sorceress Llewellyne, for example—would be up now, examining the door closely, scouring the floor for possible weapons, figuring odds, strategizing. But this wasn't Paliopolis. And she wasn't the Sorceress.

Marnie moaned, clutched her head, and slipped back into a state of unconsciousness.

CHAPTER 12

"Wake up!" said a voice that Marnie did not want to recognize. Ms. Slaight sounded sort of panicked.

Marnie kept her eyes closed. A cautious little voice in her head was wondering if she could fool Ms. Slaight into thinking she was so sick she was about to die. Which she was not. Oh, she still felt horrible—achy and dizzy. But she was better. She thought about emitting an artistic moan, tossing her head frantically, mumbling "Mommy." She felt a hand on her forehead and only just managed to keep herself from shoving it away. The little voice believed, quite forcefully, that doing so would be a bad mistake.

"Wake *up!*" said Ms. Slaight, and slapped Marnie hard across the cheek.

Marnie's eyes flew open. Involuntarily she glared at Ms. Slaight, whose face was inches from her own.

"I knew you were faking it," the woman said.

Marnie thought of several responses, including the unoriginal *You'll never get away with this!* She said nothing. She was trying frantically to recall the kidnapping lectures she'd had to listen to years ago. Something about trying to make your kidnappers like you. Since that approach was obviously doomed, she hoped she could think of another. In a day or so, she'd be stronger . . . maybe she would pretend not to be, though. And surely Max would come soon. She'd be reported missing, and then the trail would clearly lead to Ms. Slaight from the Halsett Grille. It was just a matter of time.

"You've made quite a mess," said Ms. Slaight, looking at the floor, her nostrils flaring in disgust.

Incredibly, Marnie felt abashed, even opening her mouth to apologize. But she caught herself. "I'm not feeling well," she said. The words came out in a near-croak. She cleared her throat and added recklessly: "I may die."

"You're fine," snapped Ms. Slaight. If she had been panicked before, she had gotten over it. "Even the black eye looks normal on you."

Immediately Marnie's hand was at her left eye, below the bandage. It did feel swollen, tender. She hadn't differentiated that pain from all the rest. A black eye. Well, fabulous.

Meanwhile, warily, Ms. Slaight had begun to clean up, slopping a little seltzer on the area and wiping with paper towels she'd fetched from somewhere. When she finished, she moved the Yertle bucket nearer. "There's soup here for you," she added, indicating a Thermos she'd also placed within Marnie's reach. She regarded Marnie carefully and then shrugged. Marnie thought she saw a flicker of disappointment in her eyes. "You look horrible. Go back to sleep. We can talk later." Ms. Slaight turned toward the door.

No, said the little voice in Marnie's head. It, at least, was sounding stronger. *Talk now! What kind of kidnapping is this? Doesn't she need to take a picture or video with today's paper, at least? Or is she just psycho? Please, please let her be planning a ransom note.*

Dizzily Marnie got herself up on one elbow. "Wait a minute," she croaked.

The door closed, and locked, behind Ms. Slaight. Marnie collapsed back on the cot, her mind whirling faster, now, than the room.

Marnie wasn't quite asleep, but nonetheless she dreamed. She was the Sorceress Llewellyne, alone and crouched on the dusty floor of the Lair of the Rubble-Eater.

Something was up in Paliopolis. Even the air was alert; but Llewellyne felt prepared. She carried several prizes: a fabled ruby on her left hand; a pearl-handled sword that felt very familiar in her right hand; and the spellbook warmly pulsing in her pocket. And—most precious, although quite innocuous in appearance—the truth glasses of Paliopolis dangled around her neck from a string.

There was an old tale involving the truth glasses. A curse, some said. Llewellyne was superstitious enough to be wary. She'd never yet used them.

76

All at once Llewellyne heard a cawing, and from nowhere a cyber-construct hawk materialized. She frowned at it as it hung momentarily in midair, its stylized wings outstretched. She felt she ought to recognize it. The hawk stared red-eyed back at her and then swooped to land companionably on her shoulder, mechanical toes gripping hard. The perch hurt, but she suddenly knew that the hawk *was* hers. Her partner; her friend. How could she have forgotten it?

There came a rustling ahead: the Rubble-Eater. Llewellyne pressed closer to the wall as, head down, the huge blind creature lumbered into sight. She and the hawk were downwind, so if they remained very still, it ought to be all right.

The Rubble-Eater threw itself against the far cave wall as if it thought it could break through the rock. It did this once, twice, thrice, each time attacking with greater force, each time rebounding harder, each time backing up more slowly and wincingly to try again. Throughout, there was a peculiar high-pitched sound coming from the ugly creature.

One final time, with a force that shook the entire cavern, the Rubble-Eater hurled itself against the rock wall. Not so much as a pebble crumbled off. The Rubble-Eater collapsed, trembling, onto the floor. Llewellyne hand-signaled a question to the hawk.

No, I don't have the slightest idea what that was about, the hawk thought at her. *And we haven't got time for it. We must go now. Quickly. Leave the Rubble-Eater! Who cares about it, anyway?*

Llewellyne did not obey. Instead, she groped instinctively for the truth glasses and made to train them on the now motionless Rubble-Eater.

The hawk's claws tightened.

When Marnie opened her eyes she was aware of two great needs: to pee, and to eat. Grimacing, she got up and used the Yertle bucket Ms. Slaight had left, only afterward becoming aware that she'd actually been able to stand and even squat. She moved her shoulders, arms, and legs carefully. Yes, the aches and pains were still there, but all her parts were usable. She could walk all the way to the other corner of the room and leave the bucket there. She wobbled some getting back, but that was okay. She was only feeling, as Skye would have said, a little puny.

She sat on the edge of the cot and took a swig of seltzer. Then she opened the Thermos and sniffed. Tomato soup, still relatively hot. She poured some into the Thermos's plastic cup and drank it gratefully. It tasted okay. She examined the Thermos. It was small and light, and featured an atrocious plaid pattern.

Enthroned on the cot, Marnie took stock. She had Yertle. She had the plaid Thermos. She had half a bottle of lemon-lime seltzer. She had a canvas cot. She had a blanket, seventy percent polyester, thirty percent wool; do not remove tag under penalty of law. She did not seem to have shoes, or her bag, but otherwise she was dressed as she had been at the restaurant: short black knit dress, black tights. And one black eye, of course. She suppressed a hysterical giggle.

At least you match, said the little voice in her head.

And she had her brain back. That was her mind in there, and she could feel it clicking away. Ms. Slaight wasn't so very frightening, was she? Marnie would figure something out, and soon she'd be strong enough to act. Already she had one or two intriguing ideas. Not to mention some puzzling questions, the first of which was: What did Ms. Slaight think she was doing?

We can talk later, she had said to Marnie.

There was something messed up about that. About this whole setup. You didn't have to be an heiress to have a basic understanding of kidnapping policies and procedures. Rule one was discretion, but half of Halsett had seen Ms. Slaight quarreling with Marnie at the restaurant.

Also, weren't you supposed to have a meticulous plan, with synchronized watches and alternate strategies and at least one or two accomplices in stocking masks, rather than a battered old Jetta and whatever it was that Ms. Slaight had used to conk Marnie on the head? A rock? A tire iron?

It screams improvisation, said the clear little voice in Marnie's head. *Amateur. Not to mention, the woman doesn't seem all there. . . .*

"Not to be overly critical," said Marnie aloud. "I am effectively kidnapped, after all." Her voice sounded nearly normal. That was good. She had another swig of seltzer. She pressed lightly on her forehead bandage and then explored her eye area. Only the vaguest of headaches. She was definitely going to live.

She wondered what time it was, and what day. She asked herself to guess, and decided maybe two days had passed since lunch at the Halsett Grille. Maybe it was now afternoon. Early afternoon on Thursday.

There was a rattle at the door. A key, turning in a lock? Marnie stiffened. Suddenly her skin felt too tight on her bones.

The door opened. Ms. Slaight stood in the doorway. Behind her, Marnie saw an expanse of what looked like a typical unfinished basement. Surely that was a washer and dryer at the left? Stacked boxes to the right? Before Marnie could be certain, Ms. Slaight closed the door. Marnie blinked at her. Ms. Slaight was holding a canvas folding stool in her left hand and in her right, a small gun.

Oh.

Marnie sat very still on the cot.

Ms. Slaight shook out the folding stool in front of the door and sat down on it. She rested the arm with the gun on her lap. "So," she said.

"So," Marnie echoed. She tried not to look at the gun but found her gaze drawn there anyway.

Ms. Slaight saw where she was looking. "Just in case," she explained. "I really don't want to hurt you. My having it protects both of us."

Marnie nodded, although she didn't quite see how the gun protected *her*. She ostentatiously folded her hands in her lap.

"You're feeling better, I see," said Ms. Slaight.

"Um," said Marnie, "still a little weak."

There was silence. Ms. Slaight frowned, seemingly searching for words.

Marnie controlled her breathing. If Ms. Slaight didn't understand the professional way to proceed, Marnie would help her. She began brightly: "Have you sent a ransom note yet? Maybe you'd like me to write one? You could dictate it if you want. Oh, and you ought to enclose a picture of me. Something with the date in it, to prove I'm okay. I can give you my guardian's address. No problem."

Ms. Slaight seemed a bit taken aback, and then displeased. Her forehead furrowed. Marnie thought it advisable to move on to a more attractive aspect of the conversation.

"Do you have any idea how much money you want? Five million? Ten? Why not go for a lot?"

Ms. Slaight stared. Something about her look made Marnie babble even more fluently, even as the little voice in her head began to wail, *Shut up, shut up, shut up!* "Do you have a Swiss bank account set up, or do you want small unmarked bills? I'm pretty sure Max—my guardian—will be able to handle either. If I were you I'd go for the bank. You can set up an account over the Internet if you haven't already, I'm pretty sure I could tell you how, I can give you the names of some banks—"

"Stop it," growled Ms. Slaight.

Marnie felt her jaw clamp smoothly upward and close.

"Money," said Ms. Slaight, after a moment, "is not without importance. I'd be the first to admit that. But it's not the only thing. Family is important too."

She seemed to want a response to this. Marnie attempted a nod.

Once more Ms. Slaight was frowning thoughtfully. "I would have told you this the other day. After lunch," she said. "I really would have preferred that. I had hoped we could be friends. I still hope so. Now that you're here, you'll have some time to think about things, and maybe your attitude will change. In some ways you're not really to blame. I do see that now. After all, you didn't know. You still don't."

She paused expectantly. She was looking right at Marnie. Waiting.

"Know what?" said Marnie.

"That I'm your sister," said Ms. Slaight. A timid little smile appeared on her lips. "Well, half sister, probably. I've already picked up the papers—to change my name legally and make it what it always should have been. What it rightfully should be.

"Leah Skyedottir."

CHAPTER 13

Marnie wondered if she was going to be sick again.

"I can tell you're surprised," said Ms. Slaight. "All this time at Halsett, I wondered if you would guess, but you didn't, did you?"

Marnie croaked out a syllable: "No." A clear, oddly calming thought slowly took shape in her mind: This woman was crazy.

Certifiable. Cracked. Bats in the belfry. Deranged. Unhinged. Dippy. Looney Tunes.

Ms. Slaight was smiling uncertainly. Marnie's eyes edged to the gun and then back to Ms. Slaight's face, which was full of . . . shyness. Hope. And—expectation.

Marnie's stomach turned completely over. Why was that look on Leah Slaight's face more terrifying than anything Marnie could ever have imagined?

Even when she woke up ill and cold in this place, Marnie realized, she had not truly been afraid.

In Paliopolis, the Sorceress Llewellyne could always figure a way out. There were rules. There were elves wandering around to jeer at you and steal your spellbook and otherwise keep you company. You played at fear and danger, at having courage and cunning and strength and brains . . . but it was all a game. A game.

"Maybe you should have a little water," Ms. Slaight said.

Automatically Marnie reached down for the bottle of seltzer and swallowed a very small amount.

"You really didn't guess?" said Ms. Slaight, as if she couldn't believe it. "Not even subconsciously? You didn't feel we were kin? Feel the sibling rivalry?"

Sibling rivalry. Dear God. Marnie shook her head. She put the bottle back down.

And then she did feel something. Rage. Rising, lavalike . . .

No, said the little voice frantically. *No! She has a gun. Don't be an idiot. Don't be an idiot!*

Marnie knew then, with sudden clarity, that the danger was not just this psychotic person with a gun. It was also herself. It was the way she'd been feeling lately, all untethered.

She had no idea if she could control herself.

"I think I have Skye's cheekbones," mused Ms. Slaight. "I've studied her pictures very carefully. But you and I don't look at all alike. Different fathers, I suppose."

Marnie inhaled through her nose. She clenched

her teeth against the words that battered them from behind. *You are out of your mind. You are not related to me. I am my mother's only child. Don't you speculate about my father!* She fought the rage back, down. Skye had had some wise words about self-control, but Marnie could not remember them.

"Don't you have anything to say to me? Marnie?" Ms. Slaight was looking . . . displeased? Needy? Angry?

And suddenly there was something about the way her eyes had narrowed, something about the expression deep within them, that reminded Marnie of Skye. Skye, in one of her very rare, very tightly contained rages . . .

No, she thought wildly. I'm imagining it.

Marnie choked out, "I am really—I am really in shock. I had no idea you—" But she couldn't say it. She knew she ought to, she knew it would please the lunatic, but she couldn't.

"Of course." Disappointment. "You'll need time to get used to this. I hoped, once I told you, there would be a kind of click—you know, that cosmic 'Aha!' that Skye talked about. But maybe you don't have her kind of intuition. She was deeply connected to the universe."

Marnie managed, somehow, to turn the beginning of a scream into an almost inaudible yelp. Quickly she moved her right hand behind her left forearm and began pinching her own skin, hard. The pain helped clear her head. Her little voice whispered a suggestion and she listened to it.

"Maybe . . . Do you think you could tell me the story?" she said. "How you—How you found out?"

85

"Oh," Ms. Slaight said. Her cheeks pinkened. She watched Marnie for a long moment and then nodded, as if she'd made some decision. She said slowly: "The most important thing to understand is that, from the time I was a very small child, I knew I didn't—*couldn't*—belong to the people I lived with. And I was right. I found out later I was adopted." She scowled. Her hand—unconsciously, Marnie hoped—tightened around the grip of the gun. She looked Marnie in the face again, intensely.

"I know that feeling," said Marnie quickly. "Of not belonging." She said it purely out of policy, of course, because she'd always known she *did* belong with Skye. But she was astonished at how truthful it sounded.

She saw Ms. Slaight relax a little.

"What was it about them?" asked Marnie. A little eddy of curiosity stirred inside her.

"They were . . . they were—" Ms. Slaight stopped. Her eyes went a little blank. She said softly, "When I was about your age, I heard her sing. Skye, that is. Of course it was just a recording. *Arms of the Lord.* You know that one?"

Marnie nodded cautiously. It was actually her least favorite of Skye's recordings. It was maybe disloyal of her, but the songs were so . . . so heartsick. So desolate. Late-night blues stations tended to play cuts from it long after midnight.

In fact, it had been Skye's last album. After it was released, she had unexpectedly ended her singing career, and then, at thirty-one, she had published her first book on moral philosophy. *A Spiritual Guide to Ordinary Life.*

"When I heard 'Leah,' " said Ms. Slaight to Marnie, "I knew she was singing about me." A pause, then she added flatly, "That's my name. Leah."

"Yes," Marnie said. A cold finger touched her spine. "What did you do then?" she asked inanely. She tried to remember the exact lyrics, but Skye's songwriting strength had lain in the music itself, and in her expressive voice, not in an ability to create poetic, multilayered lyrics. Still, Marnie thought she remembered some of the words:

There is no place for her
No one who cares for her
What need is there for her

The rest of the song vanished, and Marnie couldn't get it back. Meanwhile, dreamily, Ms. Slaight—Leah Slaight—was saying, "She would have been seventeen when she had me." Then she frowned. All at once she looked at Marnie the way she had when she'd been Marnie's chemistry teacher. Venomously. Involuntarily, Marnie shrank back on the cot.

"What could I do, once I realized?" said Leah Slaight bitterly. "I was sixteen. And Skye was having another baby right then. Right exactly then. You. You were the one living with Skye. You were the *Skyedottir*." She spat out the name. Then she got up abruptly and grabbed her stool. For a moment Marnie actually thought Ms. Slaight was about to hurl it at her.

Marnie's head had cleared; the anger was under

control. *What does she want from me?* she thought. *How can I make her hate me less?* She said carefully: "How could I have understood—*cared*—when I didn't *know?* I had no idea we were—you were—I don't know what to believe. . . ."

Ms. Slaight stilled. Then, slowly, she shook her head.

"Wait," Marnie said. "Wait, please." She heard the "please" with astonishment and some fear. And then she said it again. "Please. Would you at least answer a few questions?"

Ms. Slaight turned slightly—so slightly—back.

It would have to do. Marnie asked: "What day is it?"

Ms. Slaight seemed to ponder. Then she shrugged. "Friday."

Friday! Surely, surely, Max should have figured out where she was by now! Why hadn't he? What was wrong? Marnie took a deep breath. "All this stuff about Skye aside—you *are* asking for a ransom, right? That is—even if you haven't done it yet, you're going to? If you're Skye's daughter too, then you're entitled. You're entitled to half of every-thing."

For a very long moment Ms. Slaight didn't an-swer, and Marnie was filled with terror. If this wasn't about money, could not be *made* to be about money, if it was all about Ms. Slaight's crazi-ness . . . Oh, God.

But Ms. Slaight said tightly, "That's right. I've thought of that."

Marnie knew dizzying relief. She watched Ms.

Slaight go to the door. But as the woman turned the knob, Marnie heard herself call out.

"Wait! One more question, please—what are they thinking at school? Do they know I'm missing—do they know—what do they think happened to me?"

Ms. Slaight shrugged, as if it were of no concern to her at all. "Oh," she said, "it's actually a bit funny. I told them you must have run away after our fight, and they believed me. They seem to think you've gone to see someone you met on the Internet. Someone you met in that game you play.

"You're such a rebellious, irresponsible teenager," said Ms. Slaight. "Just the kind who always gets into trouble."

CHAPTER 14

Ms. Slaight left. This time, Marnie heard the distinct click of a padlock being shoved closed on the other side.

She ran to the door anyway, turned the knob, and, with all her strength, pushed, and pushed, and pushed. She heard a sound that might have been her own sobbing. Like Jenna's, the other night.

Then Marnie lost time. When she came to herself, she discovered she was wandering back and forth in the little basement room, sometimes staggering with dizziness. She had no idea how long she'd been doing this. She was cold. Her cheeks were damp. She grabbed the blanket from the bed, wrapped it around her shoulders, and kept going at a brisk, more measured pace. After a few minutes she felt warmer. She continued to walk.

Remnants of illness or not, it was time to do some serious thinking.

Yes, said the little voice firmly. *Get a grip.*

So. They thought she had run off to meet some-one from the Internet. The Elf? Must be. Well, she wished she had. In fact, she didn't dare dwell on how much she wished it. Marnie blinked hard. But *why* would they think that? Her mind spun. Had Mrs. Fisher just concocted the idea out of thin air and Marnie's old Internet statements, or did they have something more? Had they contacted Marnie's ISP and read her stored e-mails? But if that were the case, they'd have talked to the Elf by now!

Was it at all possible that Max *did* know she'd been kidnapped, but was pretending to believe the running away stuff, for investigative purposes? But if that were true, he'd have already tracked down Ms. Slaight.

By sheer will, Marnie pulled herself back from the spiraling universe of maybes and what-ifs. She took one deep breath. She sank down on the cot and took another. She imposed fierce order on her mind. She mustn't waste her time and energy on things that she had no knowledge of and no possi-bility of affecting. This was one of those rules of gaming that also applied to real life. At least, she thought it did. It made sense that it would.

One thing she knew was that Max would be out of his head, no matter what, once he knew she was missing. He'd do everything he could to find her. She could be sure of that.

Still, it was utterly stupid to pin your hopes on other people—on what they might or might not do, or say, or think. Even Max. She'd been tough on poor Max . . . maybe part of him, a secret part, felt he'd be better off without Marnie.

Almost absently, Marnie reached up and wiped her face with her palms. She exhaled. It didn't matter. It didn't matter.

Concrete reality mattered. And okay, right on schedule, here was some concrete reality to deal with: She had to use that stupid, stinking bucket. Afterward, with sudden clarity, she wondered: Why not scream? Why not yell for help? Maybe there were other houses around, with people in them, people who would hear sustained yelling and call the police. She paused, and then shook her head; it felt too risky. They had to be fairly close to Halsett, because Ms. Slaight seemed to have full knowledge of what was happening there. And Halsett was not someplace where you *knew* there were neighbors. Halsett was rural; houses were built with acres between them. But okay. Yelling. It was an option; it was a possible strategy.

It was a start.

She began pacing again. This was not Paliopolis, it was not a game, but . . . strategy was strategy. You figured out what you knew. You figured out what you didn't know. You evaluated the other players—and yourself. Then you figured your options, and for each one, the pros, cons, and risks.

Skye had written: *Even doing nothing can be an active choice.*

Yes, said the little voice in Marnie's head, *but it's not my preference.*

Okay. Marnie steered her thoughts forward.

Figure out options. Figure out players. Then strategize . . .

So. What were her options, given what she did and didn't know? So far she had one: Make a great big noisy fuss. A second, unacceptable option was to do nothing. In a bit, she'd think about others.

Now, players. Outside: Max. Halsett and its people. Max's security people. Maybe the police, the FBI. Maybe even the Elf . . .

No, said the little voice. *Wrong. Concern yourself with the players here. Inside.*

Marnie sat back down. "There are only two," she said aloud. "Leah Slaight . . ." She winced internally over the last name, hearing, in her inner ear, Ms. Slaight saying *Skyedottir*. "And me."

Really? said the voice skeptically.

"Yes." But even as she spoke, Marnie knew that was wrong.

In Paliopolis, if you overlooked an important player, you weren't just a fool. You were dead.

"Skye," said Marnie. "Present physically or not. Skye is the third player."

Yes, purred the voice in her head.

"Okay," Marnie continued aloud. "Leah Slaight is obviously one of those people who imagines she's connected to a celebrity to make herself feel important." She suddenly heard, again, the bleakness in Leah Slaight's voice. "Or . . . or just to make herself feel connected at all. But—" She stopped. Her stomach filled with a rumbling dread. Suddenly she longed to fling herself down, curl into a ball beneath the blanket, and sleep. Not think, not go down this road. Could this all be some nightmare?

It's real, said the voice, grimly. *Now go on. But what?*

After a moment, Marnie did. "But . . . ," she said slowly. "It's not that I believe her; that's ridiculous. She's based this whole fantasy on a song. The whole thing would be pathetic if—well, if I weren't here. But the thing is . . ."

A fact had appeared, crystalline, in her mind, and she faced it squarely.

The thing was, it was certainly possible for Skye to have had another child before Marnie. She had been thirty-three when Marnie was born. So, theoretically speaking . . .

Theoretically, anything is possible about Skye's early life, said that clear, cool voice in Marnie's head. At once, she recognized the voice, and was astonished that she hadn't before. The Sorceress Llewellyne. It felt utterly natural to talk to her, as if the Sorceress were separate from, as well as contained within, her own consciousness.

"No," Marnie whispered slowly to the Sorceress. "I knew Skye."

Did you really?

"She'd have told me if I had a sister."

You were only eleven when she died. She might have planned to tell you later. It's the holes in Skye's life that make Ms. Slaight's fantasy at all possible. Face it; look at the holes. . . .

But there were so many things about Skye she didn't know, Marnie thought stubbornly. There were so many holes that there was simply no point in taking the few pieces, the little she knew about Skye, and trying to make them into another picture

94

that accommodated Leah Slaight. The alternate picture of Skye was no more likely to be valid than the old one.

She stopped dead.

Yes, said the Sorceress-voice. *Exactly. The old picture is very likely to be invalid.*

That's not what I meant!

Elementary logic. Come on.

No, Marnie thought stubbornly.

You were eleven. You loved your mommy. What did you know? At least consider the possibility.

Marnie was silent. Okay, it was theoretically possible. But . . .

But suddenly, with her heart, with her mind, with her very self, she could feel Skye. She closed her eyes and saw Skye's face, felt her arms, felt her love and warmth and goodness. In her lifetime Skye had blazed so full of light that all the world had known and felt her presence. The world was a little bit different—perhaps better, kinder, more thoughtful—because Skye had lived and sung and thought and written.

Yes. Nobody's arguing with that. This is something else.

Marnie wrapped her arms around herself.

Look, you don't need to believe she did have another child, said the Sorceress-voice patiently. *You don't need to decide she didn't love you, or anything like that. You just need to acknowledge that you didn't know her. That your picture is composed of a few pieces only. You see? Don't you see? Say it out loud. It's the thing you've been running from for a long time. It's the thing you're most afraid of.*

Marnie took a deep breath. Her Sorceress-voice was trustworthy. She knew that. Whereas her own instincts . . . how often had they led her astray? She didn't know. She didn't know.

"Yes," she said finally, "it's possible." And then she added, defensively, "This doesn't mean that Leah Slaight isn't nuts. Even if I had a genetic test right here and it said—I'd still think she was out of her mind."

Yes, agreed the Sorceress. *Leah Slaight is extremely dangerous.*

"I said nuts," snarled Marnie.

And I added, dangerous, said the Sorceress quietly.

CHAPTER 15

In the hours that followed, Marnie exercised mind-over-matter discipline that she hadn't known she possessed. Except for drinking the remainder of the soup and using the odious Yertle bucket, she ignored the demands of her body. She needed to stay awake so that she could think, plan. Who knew how much time she'd have? And she'd gone without sleep many times before, hadn't she, while online? So what if, unlike Paliopolis, this particular place—the small basement room and its contents, and the three players, one of whom was a ghost—wasn't in the least fun? So what if her game-move strategies might, terrifyingly, have to be acted upon in reality?

And so what if Leah Slaight's mad claim had made Marnie Skyedottir feel as if she were a windowless house built on marshland? As if she were slipping inch by inch into some dark airless place . . .

Put it aside, said the Sorceress-voice. *Look at the options. Go over them logically.*

Marnie took inventory again. One camping cot with canvas stretched over it. One blanket. One plastic bottle of seltzer, half empty. One plaid Thermos, entirely empty.

Ah. Well, to the trained mind, the thing to do was perfectly obvious. At the first sound of Leah Slaight's key in the padlock, Marnie would emit a giant whoop and do a double back flip across the room. Her feet would hit the door with enormous impact, catapulting it open and hurling Leah Slaight (and her gun) across the basement. Marnie would land lightly beside the stunned Leah and kick the gun halfway into the next millennium.

Be serious.

Marnie buried her head in her hands.

All you really had in Paliopolis was your brain, said the Sorceress-voice, encouragingly.

After a moment, Marnie sighed deeply and sat up. She wasn't going to argue with her Sorceress-voice on that one. It was a useful lie, which was Skye's term for those personal myths that help you organize your life and keep going. And Marnie had to keep going. It was important to evaluate her position; she knew that. If—no, *when*—an opportunity arose to help herself, she had to be ready to act.

And when the wrong opportunity arises, you have to know not *to act.*

Weird, to hear the Sorceress-voice advising caution. Marnie didn't think of that part of her personality as cautious. In Paliopolis . . . But then, the Elf had been there, egging the Sorceress on, forcing her to think more quickly, more flexibly.

No. She wasn't going to think about the Elf now; it was too depressing. Except . . .

Marnie paused, considering. Except, what *would* the Elf say, if he were here in this dungeon? What would the Elf *do*?

JUMP DOWN AIRSHAFT!

Despite everything, Marnie smiled, remembering. The Elf would do something creative. Something plausible, something real, and yet . . . unexpected.

Hmm.

Careful! Leah Slaight is dangerous, said the Sorceress-voice urgently.

"I'm just going over as many possibilities as I can," Marnie said soothingly. It was amazing, she thought, how much stronger she suddenly felt. "It's all speculative."

This isn't cyberspace!

"Yeah, yeah. I know."

The Sorceress-voice subsided. In fact, Marnie could almost feel that part of her brain lean forward in interest, ready to comment, as she went over her lists again, trying to think like the Elf . . . or, rather, like the Elf-influenced Sorceress. She lifted the Thermos, and then, experimentally, hit her shoulder with it. It practically bounced off. She clicked her tongue in exasperation. The plaid unit had clearly been designed to be a safe component in a kindergarten food fight.

Could she just hurl it at Leah Slaight? And yell "Food fight?" Marnie actually grinned.

Seriously. Suppose she were to try to conk Leah Slaight on the head with—well, with something. How would she get in close enough, given that Leah was holding the gun? As Marnie had observed earlier, the door opened outward, so she couldn't hide behind it. But could she flatten herself against the wall next to the door? Would Leah Slaight be fool enough to take a couple of steps into the room even if she couldn't see Marnie? Was there enough time between the jiggling of the lock and the opening of the door for her to race across the room and position herself properly?

The Sorceress asked, *Could you make it look as if you're on the cot, covered by the blanket? Could you fluff up the blanket somehow?*

Now, that was an interesting idea, even if Marnie couldn't imagine how she'd fluff up a single blanket. It wasn't as if she had a bunch of pillows to prop underneath. Still, it was the right kind of thinking. And what about that blanket? Could it be thrown over Leah Slaight's head? Hmm. Stand still while I entangle you in my blanket. Thank you kindly.

Marnie drank a little seltzer. She wished it were in a glass bottle. Now, *there* was a weapon.

Wait, how about the seltzer itself? said the Sorceress. She was really getting into this Elf-thinking now. *If you shake an unopened bottle and then twist the cap open, it explodes all over the place. What happens if you shake a half-empty bottle?*

Marnie tried it and watched the remaining airspace in the bottle fill up with bubbles. Only partway, however. She sighed.

But if she gave you a new bottle, just like this one . . . The Sorceress was excited.

Marnie did see the potential: an explosive device. Well, sort of. But there were difficulties too. Even supposing that she did get a new bottle, how exactly would she integrate it into a realistic escape plan? Would she say: Hey, Leah, wait just a minute while I get this bottle ready to explode in your face?

Details, said the Sorceress. *They aren't important right now. You'll be improvising in the moment. Any actual plan always goes awry after step one. Or two, if you're very lucky.*

A scary thought, but Marnie knew it was accurate. It was the story of her life.

Well, then. The first step toward getting a new bottle would be to finish up this one. She took another swig. Half the bottle to go. Just thinking of it made her need to use Yertle.

Yertle. Ugh. She was almost used to breathing only through her mouth.

She kept thinking, thinking, thinking, and taking swigs of seltzer as a reward for each new idea, however loony. It turned out that there were rather a lot of things you could do with one blanket, one cot, one Thermos, and one plastic half-bottle of seltzer. Creative things. Unexpected things. But, ultimately, mostly stupid things. And while she could hear the Elf's voice insisting that stupid was good, she couldn't quite believe it.

Once more, Marnie visited Yertle. Then, finally, she let herself slip into an uneasy sleep.

* * *

In the Lair of the Rubble-Eater, Llewellyne stopped herself before she brought the truth glasses into focus on the beast. As she did so, she felt the hawk's claws ease a bit. She remembered now the old tale about the glasses; involving a young man who'd observed his lover through them and had gone quite mad. But even if that story wasn't just a fable, this was not a similar situation. The Rubble-Eater was in considerable distress. . . .

We have other things to worry about! thought the hawk urgently. Then the hawk stilled, red eyes noticing what Llewellyne, too, could see.

It couldn't be, but it was. Even after the beating the Rubble-Eater had given itself, it was stirring. It was lifting its head and sniffing the air.

It smells you, said the hawk. *Let's slip away, fast.*

But all at once, the great, strong beast was on its feet. The giant horned head swung around, and the single, tiny, blind eye fixed itself upon them.

The hawk leapt into the air, wings flapping determinedly, and landed on an outcropping of rock just above Llewellyne's head.

The Rubble-Eater emitted that peculiar, high-pitched keening. It backed up, preparatory to charging.

Reflexively, Llewellyne dropped the glasses, feeling them fall back on their string against her chest, and drew her pearl-handled sword. Then she paused.

Yes, you'll need to kill it, said the hawk encouragingly. *It's the only way we can escape now.*

Between Llewellyne's breasts, the truth glasses vibrated gently, insistently.

102

CHAPTER 16

Marnie's awareness of Leah Slaight's presence slowly filtered into her consciousness and woke her. She feigned sleep for a while, though, breathing slowly, feeling her chest rise and fall. Fear clawed relentlessly at her insides. Fear of Leah Slaight; fear of herself; fear of action; fear of inaction; fear of death; fear of—

Better stop there.

You could say a lot of things about Skye—maybe Marnie's Sorceress-voice was right and you could even call her a liar, a concealer of truths. But you would never call her a coward. If Skye could see Marnie now, trembling, what would she think of her?

Does it matter? asked the Sorceress incredulously.

Yes, Marnie thought fiercely. But then she felt a quick, deep surge of uncertainty.

That's right. To hell with her probable opinions! To hell with her!

Yes . . . no . . . yes . . .

"I know you're awake," said Leah Slaight impatiently.

Marnie skipped any artistic stretches and yawns. She opened her eyes and stared at Leah Slaight as the woman sat on her stool, gun in lap.

"Sit up," Leah said. "I want to talk to you. And have something to drink. I brought you more water. And a sandwich."

More water? Seltzer? Would it possibly be that easy? Marnie sat up slowly, swung her legs over the side of the cot, and glanced down. Yes. Yes! Another plastic bottle of seltzer; raspberry-flavored this time.

Careful, whispered the Sorceress.

Marnie picked up the bottle. How in the world would she get it ready to explode? She couldn't possibly shake it openly . . . could she?

"Have the sandwich," invited Leah.

Marnie didn't want to refuse, even though, oddly, she wasn't particularly hungry. The sandwich was peanut butter and jelly. She ate half of it while Leah watched. She thought about the seltzer. If she drank just a little, the bottle would still explode nicely. She twisted the cap open, gulped some down, and fastened the cap back into place. Suppose she *was* able to shake it up, aim it, explode it in Leah's face. What would she do afterward?

You'll run! Look, the door's ajar. This is really it! You've been so biddable, you've got her feeling overly secure.

104

Panic roiled in Marnie's stomach.

How many seconds would it take to shake the bottle, aim it? Would Leah have time to react, to evade? To aim the gun? Buying herself time to think, Marnie put the seltzer down beside her on the cot, on its side. She ate the other half of the sandwich. Each bite threatened to congeal in her mouth. Talk, Leah had said. Marnie swallowed the end of the sandwich. She focused her gaze on the top of Leah's head, noticing suddenly the shiny richness of Leah's thick brown hair. She took another small swig of seltzer, capped the bottle, and put it down again, careful to do it carelessly, shaking it.

"You have beautiful hair," Marnie said abruptly, without thinking, without smiling. She could hear the truth in her own voice and knew Leah Slaight would hear it too.

She did. Her eyes flickered in surprise. Her mouth formed a little O. Seemingly involuntarily, she put her left hand up to touch her hair. Marnie thought she could see the other hand, the one that held the gun, loosen its grip a bit.

"I do?" said Leah uncertainly.

"Yes." Marnie pushed herself forward a little, to get her feet solidly on the floor. Beside her, the bottle shifted against her body again. If she could just keep moving around on the cot so that the seltzer rolled a bit, would that shake it up enough?

"Skye was a redhead," said Leah.

"Dyed," said Marnie. "I don't know what color her real hair was. Probably brown, like mine. And yours," she added shamelessly. She was in awe at the sound of her own voice. So matter-of-fact. So calm. While inside . . .

She swayed and shifted on the cot as if to get more comfortable, and felt the seltzer roll up and down on the canvas before again settling against her side. Her stomach made a dreadful noise.

"Are you still hungry?" asked Leah. "I could bring you more soup." For someone who'd wanted to talk, she certainly wasn't in a rush to introduce her subject.

"Sure," said Marnie, even though she knew it was fear that had caused the rumbling. Right now her stomach was so tight, she didn't think she would ever have an appetite again. She picked up the seltzer bottle as if idly, and put it back down. Was that enough? She hadn't a clue.

Leah looked uneasy. "When we're done here, I'll warm some for you. Do you like chicken noodle?"

"That would be okay."

An uncomfortable silence fell. Marnie wiggled some more, and against her thigh the seltzer bottle went slosh, slosh, slosh. Marnie put her hand on it. She kept her eyes on Leah Slaight, who was fidgeting as well. Was the bottle ready to explode? Was now a good time? No. Leah was staring—

"I need a promise from you," said Leah abruptly. "I need you to swear on—on Skye's immortal soul. I'll believe you if you do that."

Oh, no, Marnie thought. She couldn't take any more Skyedottir stuff; not at this moment when she was trying to get herself ready to . . .

"What kind of promise?" Marnie asked. Her legs tensed, feet pressing on the floor. Her hand tightened on the bottle. One more good slosh, and then—

Leah leaned forward. Words spilled from her in a hectic rush. "I was thinking about what you said. About my being entitled to half of Skye's stuff. When this is over, when—if—I let you go, you have to swear you won't say it was me. Promise me that you know I'm entitled and that you'll say you never saw my face."

Marnie froze in shock, momentarily forgetting the bottle. A confusion of thoughts bombarded her.

"I can't let you go, otherwise," Leah went on urgently. "I have to think of myself. You do see that? I would like the money—I'm entitled, you're right. And maybe later on you and I could meet, and pretend to only discover then that we're sisters, and *then* I could change my name." She paused. Her eyes pleaded.

Marnie swallowed. "Oh," she managed feebly. "That's an idea. So . . . so, we'd write the ransom note together, you and I, and get you the money, and then you'd let me go, and we'd meet up later on, like in a year or two? Is that what you're thinking?"

"Yes," said Leah. "Yes!"

She is nuts, Marnie thought. If she were Leah, she certainly wouldn't trust the promise of a captive. Why, even if Marnie actually did keep the secret, there would be evidence all over the place, and did Leah Slaight think it wouldn't be suspicious if she left Halsett abruptly? Did she think the police, the FBI, whoever, were that dumb? Did she think Max wouldn't be quick to trace the ransom money?

Let's hope she is that dumb, said the Sorceress dryly.

But it wasn't just dumb, Marnie thought. It was pitiful, sad. This woman wanted a sister, a mother, so badly . . . Marnie could understand. . . .

No, don't get sympathetic! She's dangerous! Never forget that.

"I don't want to kill you," said Leah intensely. "And I would trust your word."

"You would?" Marnie's mind whirled. Was this a better option than trying to escape? Should she trust Leah, take the "do nothing" choice?

Beneath her fingers lay the bottle. She might never again have such a perfect opportunity, with Leah distracted, the door open.

Marnie wasn't conscious of thinking, of sorting through her options and choosing a particular path. She fixed her eyes on Leah's. She watched as Leah released the gun in her lap and lifted both hands in a pleading gesture. "Let's be sisters," Leah said. "For real."

This is it, urged the Sorceress. *She's not touching the gun, the door is open, the bottle is ready. Trust yourself, not her.*

"Promise me," Leah said again. "Promise me, as Skye's daughter. Promise me, on her soul." She held her empty hands out. Her eyes bore into Marnie's. "Promise me—as my sister."

I could just lie to her, Marnie thought frantically. Or I could actually keep the promise—it wouldn't make any difference. The evidence would speak for me. And if I took this risk now, if something went wrong . . .

The Sorceress was silent. She had already spoken. Marnie was on her own.

Marnie looked directly at Leah. "I promise," she said.

She watched Leah shut her eyes, in deep emotion.

And in that moment, Marnie lifted the seltzer bottle, gave it a final, sharp shake, and, in one beautiful flow of movement, leapt to her feet, untwisted the cap, and aimed the bottle opening directly at Leah.

CHAPTER 17

The seltzer exploded even more spectacularly than Marnie had hoped, showering everything in a 270-degree arc centered on Marnie's hands. Moving forward in the same instant—a bare second before Leah yelped—Marnie threw the bottle forcefully in the direction of Leah's head and sprinted toward the door.

Go for the gun, go for the gun! yelled the Sorceress, but Marnie didn't pause. She grabbed the door and flung it wide. *Shut her in, then!* demanded the Sorceress, and Marnie wasted a precious moment grabbing the knob and slamming the door behind her. In the very next second she heard the padlock fall to the floor and bounce out of arm's reach. There wasn't time to grab it, get it back into place, close it, lock Leah in. Marnie's chest rose and fell. Suddenly and with utter clarity, she knew the Sorceress had been right: she should've thrown herself on top of

110

Leah and tried to grab the gun. Five seconds ago, it had seemed the riskier choice.

Too late now.

Leah was screaming actual words. Instinctively, Marnie threw herself back against the door in the same moment that Leah grabbed the knob on the other side to push the door open. Marnie dug her heels into the rough floor and gritted her teeth, holding the door closed with her body. Then, behind her, Leah crashed against the door, skidding Marnie forward an inch or two. Marnie shoved back, managing to force the door shut again. She could hear Leah retreat, preparatory to another slam. She braced herself.

Leah was taller and heavier than Marnie. Marnie didn't need the Sorceress to tell her that all the laws of physics were on Leah's side.

Once more, Leah slammed against the door. It pulsed. Grimly, Marnie hung on.

She looked frantically around and saw an escape route only a few yards away: a wooden staircase leading upward. Three seconds to get to it, another four to sprint to the top. Once she got outside, her chances would surely be better.

Slam.

It was harder, this time, to push back. Marnie knew she couldn't handle many more of these. She scanned the area again. Was there something she could quickly shove against the door? She saw some old wooden two-by-fours, paint cans, an ancient microwave oven, a big overstuffed lounge chair against the far wall. Yes!—no, she could never push the chair into place in time. Refastening the padlock was a better idea, but could she do it quickly enough? She knew the answer was no.

Slam.

Marnie panted. The soles of her heels, braced against the floor, hurt horribly. She simply could not get through more than a couple more of these assaults. In fact, Marnie thought distinctly, if Leah abandoned the run-and-jump technique and merely pushed for a sustained two minutes, it would all be over.

She moved from the door and grabbed up a two-by-four.

One . . .

Two . . .

Three—

Slam!

Screaming, Leah hurtled through the door, right shoulder first, right hand holding the gun at her side. She was moving fast, expecting a resistance that wasn't there, and ran past Marnie.

Marnie swung the two-by-four. It connected solidly with Leah's shoulders. Leah staggered but didn't fall. Didn't drop the gun.

Her head, why didn't you aim at her head? wailed the Sorceress. *Try again, try again!*

Marnie felt sick. The Sorceress was more violent than she was. How could she physically aim at someone's *head*? This wasn't Paliopolis; it was real and she couldn't—

Leah had swiveled around, her eyes wild with rage, with fear, with—betrayal. She raised her gun arm.

Marnie became aware that she, too, was screaming. Heart in throat, she took a frantic step back and swung the two-by-four again. Low. The end of the two-by-four collided with the underside of Leah's right hand, forcing it upward along with the gun it clutched. Marnie backed up and lashed out again.

The gun went flying sideways through the air across the room, smacking against the far wall and falling behind the lounge chair. Marnie gasped. Her eyes locked with Leah's. Leah's body blocked the way to the staircase. The gun was about equidistant from both of them.

Leah bolted for the gun.

Dropping the two-by-four, Marnie raced for the stairs. She ran the five-yard dash of her life. She had enough time to get away, to get out; she knew she did. Gaining the foot of the stairs, she reached out and grabbed the railing and used it to swing her body around and onto the staircase without losing momentum. Her feet pounded up the stairs. One, two, three, four, five—

With terrific force, she collided into someone who'd been racing down the stairs even more rapidly than she'd been racing upward. He—it was a he—yelled something, as, once again, the laws of physics spoke decisively in Marnie's disfavor.

She landed painfully, tangled with the tall newcomer in a heap at the bottom of the stairs. They lay, stunned, for several seconds too long. Marnie knew it. She felt the vital moments tick away as she got her wind back.

She waited for sounds from above. Police sirens. Shouts. Someone who was with this stranger who'd collided with her. Tentative hellos. Anything.

Nothing came.

Leah said, in a voice that shook: "I've got the gun."

Marnie examined the newcomer's shocked face, so close to hers. Unless they were recruiting teenagers, he couldn't possibly be a member of the police or the FBI. A neighbor who'd heard the ruckus? An accomplice of Leah's?

No, said the Sorceress slowly. *Not Leah's accomplice. Not a neighbor.*

"If either of you moves," said Leah, "I'll kill you."

Marnie didn't move. Neither did the young man. He was a little older than her, Marnie guessed. The shaved head definitely did not add to his looks. He was nobody's idea of gorgeous. Except—except for his eyes.

"Sorcer—Marnie?" he said. "Marnie, it is you, right? I heard screaming. Sorry—are you all right?"

Sorcer.

You know who this is, said the Sorceress.

It was impossible. It was completely and utterly impossible. And yet, on another level, it seemed completely natural. Of course he would show up. He always did, lately.

Marnie felt her mouth shape itself into a bitter little smile. "Hello, Elf," she said.

CHAPTER 18

"Sorceress," said the Elf, formally, with a duck of the head that in any other situation might have been gallant. Here, now, sprawled and entangled at the bottom of a flight of basement stairs, it was merely preposterous. Marnie felt an incipient bubble of hysteria. Then, anxiously, the Elf said again: "Marnie? Are you okay?" And hearing the cadence of his voice, Marnie thought foolishly: Oh.

Oh, it's you.

"I'm just fabulous," she heard herself say.

She had landed mostly on top of the Elf. Beneath her palms, Marnie could feel his heartbeat, accelerated from running and from the fall. Their eyes met. Marnie's heart performed an involuntary gymnastic contortion.

"Get up!" Leah Slaight's voice slashed across Marnie's thoughts. "Both of you." As if she felt she

115

needed to repeat it, Leah added shrilly: "I've got the gun."

Marnie kept her eyes on the Elf's face, which had gone very white. "I don't suppose you're with an undercover teenage SWAT team," she said to him.

The Elf shook his head. His lips formed words that didn't come out. They might have been, *I'm sorry*.

"Not criticizing, just checking," Marnie babbled. "You never know. People aren't always what they seem—"

"Now!" barked Leah, who had evidently seen many police movies.

The Elf's shoulders raised in the tiniest of shrugs, and it was as if the small movement restored something of Marnie to herself. Awareness of a couple of new aches penetrated. Her right elbow, in particular. She blinked and looked away from the Elf. Carefully she levered herself off him and onto her knees. For the first time since the running collision, she raised her eyes and looked fully at Leah Slaight.

Leah was six feet away, fixed in a bent-leg stance with both hands on the gun. Her face looked as if it was molded from melted wax. Her eyes were pieces of flat black coal. The mouth of the gun, too, was a single large black eye. Leah was listening intently, and Marnie knew instinctively that she was trying to hear whether anyone else was coming. Someone who might have come with the Elf. Police, maybe.

The silence elongated. Only a few seconds, yet it seemed to last forever.

"You too," said Leah to the Elf, more quietly than before. "Get up."

116

The Elf lifted his torso from the floor and then paused, leaning on his elbows. Thankfully distracted from Leah, from the awful silence, Marnie frowned down at him. Had he just winced? His lips were tight.

"Are you okay?" she asked him. This time her voice came out sounding almost squeaky. She could feel the gun, its eye, staring at her. No. At them.

The Elf succeeded in rolling to his side. He reached down to touch his ankle and winced again, clearly in pain. A single sentence formed itself in Marnie's consciousness, in illuminated letters.

We are both going to die.

With the sentence came an inchoate rush of emotions. She had been escaping. In fact, if the Elf hadn't come barreling down the staircase she'd surely have made it away! And now he was hurt, and in danger too, and it was all her—no, it was his own stupid, stupid fault! If he hadn't been so fast down the stairs, if—he was always messing her up, always! This was not Paliopolis—and, oh, now, *now*, she couldn't stand it if he too—

"I need a little help getting up," said the Elf. He had turned his head and was speaking directly to Leah; speaking calmly, matter-of-factly, and with an unobtrusive note of courtesy. "Can Marnie help me? Would that be okay? It's my ankle." As if he were conversing at a party, he added: "Typical. I'm kind of clumsy. My mother says it's because my feet are too far away from my head."

"Who are you?" said Leah. Her voice was not steady, but the mouth of the gun was. Very. "What are you doing here?"

Marnie stilled. Yes, she'd like to know the answer to that second question, too.

"I'm a friend of Marn's," said the Elf, again in that calm, conversational tone. "Some people came to my house a day or two ago, thinking she might've been planning to visit me. I knew she hadn't, so I figured I'd drive up here and look around. See if I could find her." In his voice Marnie heard the lingering amazement that he had, in fact, found her.

And wait a minute. What had he just called her? Marn? Rhymes with barn? Eww.

"No," Leah said impatiently. "Why—how—did you come *here*?" She gestured around the basement.

"Well, first I went to Halsett with my buddy Dave," the Elf said, as if it were an entirely reasonable thing for him to have been doing, as if this were an answer.

Without Marnie's assistance, the Elf slowly, deliberately, heaved himself onto one knee. He grimaced and, automatically, Marnie shifted closer and offered him a shoulder and arm. Favoring his left leg, he leaned on her as they struggled upright. He was heavier than he looked. And at least a foot taller than Marnie.

She felt small and delicate.

More or less vertical now, the Elf shifted his attention—and that calm, calm voice—back to Leah. He smiled suddenly, moronically, right at her. "So when this girl said Marn had been having lunch with you before she took off, I decided to come talk to you. You are Ms. Slaight, right?"

Leah was shaking her head. "No," she said. "No!"

Her knuckles whitened on the gun, and simultaneously Marnie felt her own hand tighten on the Elf's arm.

"No?" said the Elf. "But isn't this—" Suddenly he had fished a small piece of paper from his jeans pocket. "—R.R. 1, Number 107, Back Nippin Road?" He looked up inquiringly. "Home of Leah Slaight, chemistry teacher?"

In that moment Marnie stopped trying to second-guess him. She had no idea where he was going with this. But she was suddenly sure that he was going somewhere. She knew him; he would have a plan—

She went back to listening. She had missed something.

"So, the thing is," the Elf was saying earnestly to Leah, "people know where I am. They knew I was coming out here to see you. And actually, my friend Dave just dropped me off here. He'll be back shortly."

For a moment, Marnie's heart leapt with belief. She saw Leah's gun waver. She saw doubt bloom on that waxen face.

The Elf wasn't paying any attention to Marnie now. He had actually taken a small step—well, a limp—toward Leah. He was looking straight at her.

"So I have an idea," said the Elf calmly. "I think Marnie and I should just leave here now. I figure we go back to the school, and pretend that Dave and I just dropped her off there. That she ran away, just like they think. And we forget that anything else ever happened. Just . . . forget about it."

No way she'll go for *that,* thought Marnie. But she discovered she was holding her breath.

"Ms. Slaight?" said the Elf. "What do you think?" His voice was soft now. "We just all shake hands and, well, go home. We get a good night's sleep, and tomorrow, wake up to a new day."

So soft, that voice. So clear. So reasonable.

Was Leah listening? Did she believe? Maybe. Maybe. She was frowning . . . and earlier, she'd wanted to believe that she and Marnie could be sisters, that she could trust Marnie. Maybe she'd want to believe a second time . . . maybe she was unbalanced enough . . . needy enough . . .

But then it happened.

"Dave will be back soon," repeated the Elf, and it was probably something about how he said it. Perhaps it simply came out too quickly. Perhaps he shouldn't have said anything at all, but merely let the silence sit. It hardly mattered. In one instant there had been hope. In the next it was gone.

The Elf was no fool. He heard the change in the air. Marnie actually felt his realization in his body, through her hand on his arm. She heard the tiny exhale of dismay.

"You're lying," said Leah Slaight to the Elf, and the words rushed out of her fiercely. "You're as much of a liar as she is!"

The Elf moved. Marnie would never understand exactly what he thought he'd accomplish. She felt him shift, and then all at once he was a step closer to Leah, in front of Marnie.

And a shot rang out.

Marnie screamed. The Elf crumpled to the floor.

CHAPTER 19

Never would Marnie have believed that she would welcome being locked back into the basement cell. But her relief was enormous, if momentary. No matter what Leah might do later, the Elf was alive now. Leah's shot had hit him in the right thigh; he was in no serious, no immediate, danger. And neither, incidentally, was Marnie. It was a miracle. She felt the blood pulsing in her veins as it never had before; she was alive, alive. And yet . . .

She shivered. As if pulled, she went back to the door and listened for a moment. Silence; the kind that spoke emphatically of the lack of human presence beyond. For the sake of thoroughness, Marnie grasped the doorknob firmly and turned it, pushing hard at the door. Oh yes, the padlock was back in place. And despite Leah's assault on the door itself during Marnie's abortive escape attempt, it felt no less sturdy than it had an hour ago.

She exhaled audibly. Behind her, she could hear the Elf's breathing as he lay on the cot. She glanced back at him, saw his chest rise shakily and then fall. They had managed to do a kind of three-legged stagger across the floor to reach the cot, and Marnie had had to kick the half-empty seltzer bottle out of their path. It had rolled off, its mouth trailing more water across the floor. Somehow the sight of it had made Marnie even more queasy.

Marnie's hand left the doorknob and rose to her cheek.

It was as if part of her mind were aerially posed over a maze, looking down on herself and the Elf, trapped inside. She could see all possible avenues of action. Every cul-de-sac, every dead end, every blind alley, every trap. But no way out.

Marnie turned her back on the locked door. She looked at the Elf. At the seltzer bottle. She found she had wrapped her arms around herself.

"Marn. You—okay?" The syllables came out of the Elf in little puffs. He was trying to sit up; his forehead was furrowed.

Marnie crossed the room in three strides. She knelt by the side of the cot. "I'm fine. Be quiet for now, Elf, all right? Concentrate on breathing."

He eased back down, his keen eyes only half open. For the first time Marnie noticed his ridiculous camouflage clothes. And those combat boots! When you added in the bald head, he was the perfect picture of a thug. The kind of kid adults called the police about. Marnie remembered Jenna Lowry's clean-cut hockey boy and repressed a bubble of hysterical laughter. It just went to show—actually, she wasn't sure what it went to show. Something. Nothing.

First things first. "Are you in a lot of pain?" she asked.

He shook his head. "It's not bad," he said, and she recognized the lie in his voice. For the first time it occurred to her that the Elf had thus far behaved like some macho hero stereotype. He hadn't even yelled when Leah shot him. Who did he think he was, some cyberspace adventurer with ten virtual lives? The Elf, for real?

"Listen," he said. He was making an effort to talk in a normal rhythm rather than in gasps. "I'm an idiot. I want you to know I know that. I heard screaming. I should have gone back to the car, called the police on the cell phone—but I—somehow I just knew it had to be you. I didn't think past helping you. I just ran toward the screaming." His lips twisted. "Real smart. Like the girl who gets knocked off in the first five minutes of a horror movie."

"It'll be okay," Marnie said automatically. "Just try to relax while I—"

"You think it'll be *okay*?" He sounded incredulous.

"Yeah," said Marnie. "Somebody besides you is sure to show up here, right? If you found your way to Leah, somebody else will too. Max—he's my guardian. Or someone."

"I met Max," the Elf said. "I talked to him—he thought maybe you were with me. He asked me who else you hung out with in Paliopolis. No one, I said. That I knew of. But I said I didn't know everything. Didn't really know you."

The Elf had opened his eyes fully now. They met Marnie's without evasion, searching. "Although," he added, "I feel like I do. Almost."

Marnie looked back. She looked directly into his eyes, and for a moment she felt as if he could see what she saw, know what she knew, fear what she feared. And those eyes. The lashes were almost enough to compensate for the bald head—

The world tilted terrifyingly on its axis.

Suddenly, oddly, the Elf was smiling. "You know, I don't believe we've actually been formally introduced—"

No, Marnie thought. The word came up in a desperate cry inside her. *No!* She wrenched her gaze away. "Elf," she interrupted, "I don't have time for that stuff, okay? I need to look at the gunshot area. And that ankle." Her voice came out too loud, too flip, and she cringed inside, even as another part of her settled down, appeased but wary, watching, on guard.

There was a little pause. The Elf seemed puzzled. He said, "Okay."

Marnie took a deep, relieved breath. "Okay," she said, and lifted her chin. "Ankle first. It's the left one, right?"

Thankfully, the Elf turned his face away, to look toward his ankle. "Yeah." A little too quickly, he added, "I'm sure it's just a sprain," and Marnie felt her lips tighten. Please. Who was he trying to impress? Abruptly, and for some reason she didn't care to examine, Marnie yanked hard on the Elf's left combat boot.

As it turned out, Mr. Macho Cyberspace Hero had a satisfyingly loud yell, when you took him by surprise.

CHAPTER 20

It *was* most likely a sprain, Marnie thought, when—more gently—she got the boot off. The Elf's ankle was swollen badly, but at least to Marnie's tentative, embarrassed fingers and eyes there was no sign of an actual break. His breathing became a little harsher, but she had no idea what he was really feeling; after that first squawk he had reverted to his Cyberspace Hero imitation.

"Okay," Marnie said a little too briskly. "Let's move on to the bullet wound. Do you think you could roll onto your side, so I can see the back of your other leg?"

The Elf succeeded in rolling so that he faced away from Marnie. Marnie got her first complete look at the gunshot wound and her stomach cramped. Oh, God. A long gully of flesh seemed to have gouged right out of the Elf's leg. The wound had bled freely—he had left a trail across the floor a few minutes ago—but now the blood appeared to be congealing. Marnie thought that was a good sign. She hoped it was. She was pretty sure the shot hadn't hit an artery, or there'd be spurting blood . . . or he'd be dead.

"What's with the camouflage shorts?" she asked, mostly to distract him, and herself. The Elf was twisting, trying to get a look at the back of his leg, and she thought that was a bad idea. "What's with the shorts, period? It's cold out—it's only April."

To her surprise, he stopped squirming. "It's what I wear," he said.

What if the bullet was still in there? Marnie uttered a brief silent prayer and then touched the gully cautiously. Then she pressed firmly. The Elf recoiled but still didn't, wouldn't, yell again.

Marnie honestly didn't think there was a bullet. She sent up a quick hallelujah. "Not very fashionable, camouflage," she commented, wondering what she could use for a bandage.

The Elf was silent.

"Do you realize you look like some kind of nutcase skinhead? With the boots and all, that is." Should she try to tear up the blanket? Or squirm out of her own tights and use part of them as a bandage? She could rip them with her teeth.

The Elf was still silent. Marnie regarded his back thoughtfully. He was in a cotton T-shirt, in that same combat green camouflage, and she liked the idea of using cotton, but that would leave him half naked in this cold room. What if she managed to tear a strip off the bottom of the T-shirt? Then he could put it back on and wrap up in the blanket—

which would never cover his legs; he'd need to curl up . . . But wait, the ankle should be elevated, right?

The Elf was still silent.

"You okay?" said Marnie.

"Yeah."

"Cleaning," Marnie said softly to herself. Her eyes flicked to the floor, to the abandoned, half-empty seltzer bottle. She stared at it. Her mind worked grimly. Fact: The wound had to be cleaned. Raspberry seltzer probably wasn't very antiseptic, but what were her choices?

"I'm not, you know," said the Elf abruptly.

"Not what?" The only alternative Marnie could think of was spit, and no sooner had she had the thought than she cringed. She picked up the seltzer bottle. About a third of the liquid was left. She had a feeling that spit was a better idea. Wasn't animal saliva antiseptic? Was human?

Kiss it and make it better, whispered the Sorceress mockingly.

Marnie's throat suddenly felt very dry. She swallowed.

"Not a nutcase skinhead. Not a skinhead at all," said the Elf.

It took Marnie a moment to recall the conversational thread. "Oh," she said. "I didn't think you were. It's just, you know, how you look." She suddenly knew that it didn't matter if spit was a better idea. She didn't care if they both died; she was *not* going to spit up all over the Elf's leg.

"I would never have guessed *you* cared about appearances," he said.

Marnie stilled. Incredibly, her mind emptied of all thoughts of antiseptics and water supplies. Of Leah's possible actions and inactions. Of how Max could be so stupid, thinking she'd run off to meet someone she'd only ever met online. Her hand went to her cheek.

All at once she was hideously conscious of her body. She had been here for days. *Days.* Her hair. Her makeup. This dress she'd slept in, that she'd never liked anyway . . . and the bump on her head . . . and her black eye . . . and—she must *reek.* Speaking of which—oh, God. Yertle. Over there. She couldn't smell it anymore herself. But she knew he would. He must. Right now, even. Right *now.*

Yertle.

Marnie stood there, frozen in the silence, holding the bottle of seltzer, and she wished there were an airshaft, with certain death at the bottom, that she could dive into. That would be infinitely easier.

Hold on, whispered the Sorceress-voice. *Hold on.*

Marnie breathed.

"Listen, Elf, I have to clean your leg," she said finally. "I'm going to use some seltzer for that. And then I think I should use part of your shirt for a bandage. Okay?"

"Sure," said the Elf. All she saw was his back.

"Okay, then," mumbled Marnie.

In silence, somehow, together, they got his shirt off. He was painfully skinny. Stubbornly she emptied her mind of everything else and worked. It hurt him. But she did a pretty good job, she thought. The wound *looked* clean. She had used fully half of

the remaining seltzer, fiercely ignoring the knowledge that this was their only water supply, and had
let him drink another inch of it.

"Thank you," he said quietly.

She tried to get him to wrap up in the blanket,
but he refused. "You use it," he said.

But she wouldn't either. He looked at her. She
looked back.

She would get used to the eyes. You could get
used to anything.

"Now," croaked the Elf, "will you please tell me
what's going on? What's with that woman?"

Marnie gathered her wits. "You first," she said. A
slew of questions swelled within her. "There isn't
really a buddy Dave in some car, right? It was so
obvious you were lying to Leah—"

"I wasn't lying," said the Elf defensively. "There
is a Dave. My friend David. I did come in his car."
He paused. "He's just, uh, not here with me. It's
school break for us, too, and his parents took him
off to some Caribbean island, end of last week. He
loaned me his car, and I drove up to Halsett in it
this morning. I was worried about you. I don't
know what I thought I could do, but . . ." He tried
to sit up, and his face whitened.

"You all right?" Marnie asked quickly. Deep inside, she was riveted by his words. He'd been worried about her? But he didn't even know her!

"Yeah." The Elf eased himself back down. He
threw an arm up to hide his expression. Plainly, he
wasn't all right. "Would you please sit?" said the Elf,
gesturing somewhat wildly with the other arm
toward the end of the cot.

130

Sit? On the cot? With him? Marnie's stomach performed an unexpected double flip. She surreptitiously lowered her head and sniffed herself. Nothing, which proved only that her nose wasn't working.

The Elf waited.

Finally, gingerly, Marnie sat down at the foot of the cot, a careful few inches from the Elf's long legs, with her back against the wall. By turning her head to the left, she could see the Elf. If she looked straight ahead, however, she didn't have to see him at all. Or know if he was looking at her. An excellent option.

"Could you just tell me your whole story?" she asked uncomfortably. "Everything about how you ended up here? The meeting with Max—everything from when we didn't e-mail each other."

For answer, the Elf threw the blanket toward her. After a second she understood that she would have to wrap herself in it before he would talk. She put it over her legs, and his. She squirmed. She glanced at the Elf, and against her will, flushed.

"Okay," said the Elf, after another second. "Here goes."

CHAPTER
21

"Well," the Elf began, "you'd said you'd be on-line at midnight Monday. And of course you weren't. I e-mailed you twice, and then I checked Paliopolis in case I'd misunderstood and we were supposed to meet there." As he talked, he grimaced slightly and began rubbing at the T-shirt strip that Marnie had bound around his leg, and Marnie's worry about their lack of antiseptic resurfaced. But his expression was far away, in his story, and the rubbing appeared to be an unconscious reflex, so she decided not to ask if it was hurting. Besides, she knew the answer. How could it not hurt?

"I even looked in on the Rubble-Eater, just in case you'd set a trap there or something," the Elf had continued. He grinned at Marnie, and she found herself smiling a little, shaking her head ruefully. It *was* the kind of thing that she—the Sorceress—might have done.

All at once it was astonishing how comfortable Marnie felt, sitting with the Elf, listening to him. Something in her, that was nearly always tense in the company of other people, seemed to dissolve. Unconsciously, Marnie curled her legs beneath her and leaned infinitesimally closer. The Elf had that inward look on his face that people get sometimes when they tell stories, so she even found it okay to watch his face, the play of expression, as he spoke.

He said, "It took a day or so, actually, before I started feeling antsy about not hearing from you. At first I thought you'd just gotten caught up in something or other. It happens. So I e'd you again Wednesday afternoon. And then I thought maybe I'd pissed you off in some way. I, uh, I tend to piss people off a lot."

"You do?" Marnie was surprised, then intrigued. "How?" Involuntarily, her eyes slid to his bare scalp, and he noticed. He turned away a little, and Marnie remembered that when they'd touched on his appearance earlier, he'd sounded kind of defensive, and he—

"I assume you want only *relevant* facts?" said the Elf.

—was still defensive. Okay, fine. "Right," said Marnie. "So you e'd me on Wednesday afternoon." She frowned. "Actually, why'd you do that? You knew I wasn't responding to e-mail. If I was going to e you back, I would have already."

"Yeah. I don't know! I just e'd you, okay?" He

looked down. "Well, you'll find out anyway, if we get out of here. Which I believe we will. I, uh—the fact is, I e'd you a lot on Wednesday."

Marnie was fascinated. "Define 'a lot.'"

Silence. Then: "Fifteen times. Not that I was counting."

Marnie felt her jaw drop. She stared.

After a few seconds, the Elf began to babble. "Well, the first time was just to ask you to e me back. Then, well, I sent you something. Then I figured you were offended, so I apologized." He scowled. "*You* try writing an apology when you're not sure what you did wrong! And then I got a little worried, so I e'd about that, just to tell you to say you were alive, if nothing else. They all just added up, okay?"

"To fifteen?" said Marnie. She, herself, had only counted to four. An unexpected giggle threatened to come out of her mouth. Perhaps the Elf was doing some kind of advanced math.

There was a silence. Then the Elf said, "Assuming we get out of here, I don't suppose you'd be willing to trash them without reading them?"

Now was not the time for laughing, Marnie thought. The Elf would think she was laughing at him. Which she was not. Oh, she was not. The Elf was looking down again. She wanted to say something, but she didn't know what, or how. She just felt . . . thought . . . felt . . .

Oh, she was tired of trying to figure out what it was she felt. She didn't know anything anymore. Except one thing, maybe.

"No way am I deleting those messages," she said aloud.

The Elf didn't respond. Marnie wanted to look at him closely, to try to figure out what he was thinking, but even more strongly, she didn't want to.

"And then your guardian Max showed up at my house on Thursday morning," the Elf went on steadily. He had evidently recovered from his momentary embarrassment about the e-mail. "With some weedy guy who'd apparently been reading your online records as if they were a public Web site."

That riveted Marnie. Burglarizing her online records! She had to squash down sudden, fierce indignation. Of course she wanted Max and a huge team of experts investigating her disappearance. Of course she did. It was their best hope. But oh, how she squirmed to think of them reading her stuff!

"And there was a big guy who never said who he was," continued the Elf. "Looking at me like I had an arsenal of weapons stowed in the garage and was planning to blow up my high school on Adolf Hitler's birthday." He grimaced.

"Huh," said Marnie. She thought it likely that the Elf got a lot of that kind of suspicion from people. He was certainly asking for it. She wondered suddenly if that was what Mrs. Fisher and the dean had been thinking about her. She gritted her teeth.

Then she noticed that the Elf was still rubbing his leg. "It's hurting?"

His hand froze. "No, no. Not much." And suddenly Marnie was once again aware of the fact that he was only inches away. Too close. Looking straight at her again. She'd been more comfortable when he was a glyph on a screen; that was an utter, absolute fact. And yet . . .

"Stop looking at me so hard," Marnie found herself saying. And then added, out of nowhere: "You don't know anything about me."

"Right," said the Elf. He was looking very calm, very intent. "That was made very plain to me." Marnie found she couldn't meet his eyes. After another minute, he went on talking.

It seemed that Max and his team were systematically questioning anyone who'd encountered Marnie in cyberspace at all. "I got pinpointed for special treatment because of all the e-mail," said the Elf. "But after a couple of hours I think they believed me, that we'd only ever talked online, and that I hadn't seen you. I did volunteer to take a lie detector test. But anyway, nobody thought I'd kidnapped you or anything like that." He frowned. "They seemed pretty certain you'd run away, Marn. Nobody implied anything else. In the end they just told me to contact them if I heard from you." He paused. "But what I don't understand—this *is* a kidnapping, not a runaway situation. So why don't they know that? Hasn't there been a ransom note?"

"I guess not," said Marnie.

"Why not?" asked the Elf bluntly.

Marnie met his eyes.

"That woman is nuts," said the Elf. It was part statement, part question. "This is a kidnapping, but not an ordinary one?"

Marnie nodded.

"Tell me," said the Elf.

Marnie opened her mouth and then closed it. She looked down, at a loss. How could she explain? It was such a mess. Such an embarrassing mess. And some bits—the parts about Skye—were so very private. She thought of Leah's intensity. *Skyedottir.* Of her own newly reinforced awareness of how little she knew about Skye. She thought of her own mistakes, her temper . . . Finally she said, feebly, "It's a long story."

The Elf didn't reply immediately, and at last Marnie had to look at him. Somehow he had managed to prop himself up on an elbow. "Oh, sorry," he said. "I'm just having trouble deciding which sarcastic comment to make. I'd almost decided to go with the one where I explain that I've been working to improve my short attention span."

Marnie's lips tightened. She thought seriously about kicking the Elf right in the gunshot wound.

"Well?" demanded the Elf. "Are you going to tell me what happened here? How you got here?"

"After you finish telling me your part." That would buy her time. And she did want to know.

"Fair enough," said the Elf after a moment.

Marnie took in a shallow breath, feeling reprieved, even though the Elf was still looking at her and she wished he would stop. Eventually, he did go on with his story. He had wandered around the Halsett campus, "checking things out," until he eventually met a girl who'd been willing to chat, first about the campus and then about other things. From her, he had heard the latest school scandal, the tale of Marnie's running away to meet someone she knew online. Idly, Marnie wondered who he'd talked to. Jenna? Since it was break, there weren't many students around.

"The thing that bugged me both times I heard that story," said the Elf, "is that . . . well, I suppose I can see how someone might think it could be true. And okay, even though you hadn't come to see me, I suppose you might be friendly with ten different people online, who knows? But . . ."

"What?"

"But I just didn't believe it," he finished. "In Paliopolis, you know every trap and scam there is. You wouldn't just take off to see some stranger you only knew online."

You did, Marnie thought suddenly. Sort of. Although it was different, she knew. The things boys felt comfortable doing. Like it or not. Even reasonable or not. But she kept her mouth shut and listened to the rest of the Elf's story.

"She—this girl—told me you'd had lunch with a teacher before you ran away. So I just thought I'd talk to the teacher. I got her address from the phone book, but no one answered when I knocked. I was just kind of looking around outside her house when I heard the screaming." He shrugged, then winced, and Marnie's hands clenched; she knew he was in worse pain than he was letting on. It was only then that she fully took in what he'd just said. And remembered—he'd said it earlier as well.

"Wait. I'm in the basement of Leah Slaight's actual house?" Marnie couldn't believe Leah could be so stupid. On the other hand, maybe it wasn't stupid. No one but the Elf had come, after all.

"Yeah," said the Elf. "Get this: She hadn't even locked the front door."

Marnie looked at the Elf. He was frowning. And then he opened his mouth. "So here's the real question. If I could find you—okay, I wasn't looking, exactly, but I did find you—why haven't they? This Max and his bunch of experts. I'm smart, I'm not putting myself down. To tell you the truth, I think highly of my own brains. But I'm not a trained detective, and I don't get why everybody is off chasing this Internet illusion, and not reality. When even I could guess that you would never . . ."

Hearing the question aloud, Marnie knew the answer. It appeared, not in words, not in her brain, but in her heart. She bit her lip.

My fault, said the Sorceress quietly. *All that online stuff laid a false trail.*

No, Marnie replied forcefully in her head. Not your fault. Mine. Years of not talking to Max at all . . . She faltered. She sat in silence.

The Elf didn't say anything for a long time either, clearly pursuing his own train of thought. Then he asked gently: "Are you close to this guy Max? You, uh, you trust him?"

"He's okay." Marnie knew it sounded feeble. She was still reeling from what she'd just understood.

The Elf was quiet again. Marnie knew just what he was implying. It made perfect sense, if you didn't know Max. Or Skye. Or the whole situation. "Look, Elf," she said. "Max isn't in on this. He's out there trying his best."

"I don't want to offend you. But you're sure—"

"Yeah," said Marnie. And she was. "Max has his

139

faults, but he's okay. He's trying hard. And he may get here yet. I—I think he will." She hoped so.

She could feel the Elf's gaze.

"Max won't let Skye down if he can help it," Marnie said, and heard the truth—and the emptiness—in the flatness of her own voice.

A pause. Then: "But Skye's dead," said the Elf, slowly, as if he hadn't wanted to speak it but couldn't avoid doing so.

"Doesn't matter," said Marnie. And suddenly she found herself saying something else, something she hadn't even realized she knew. "Max loved Skye. She liked him; she trusted him. They were friends. But she didn't love him back. She didn't love anyone but me. For all her talk about love, she couldn't. Not that way." Marnie stopped.

The Elf waited.

"But Max loved her, and he still does. It's a stronger tie for him than I can even understand, I think. And that's one reason why he—" Marnie stopped.

Why he keeps trying to take care of Skye's daughter, whispered the Sorceress-voice. *Who can't let anyone get close. Just like her mother.*

CHAPTER 22

A silence fell, and elongated, and Marnie was once
more filled with the realization that the Elf was
a stranger. And here she was, telling him things
that she herself didn't fully comprehend.

She chanced a sidelong glance at his face; he was
looking quietly back at her. He nodded acknowl-
edgment of what she'd said about Max, but didn't
say anything else and she was overcome by gratitude. She shivered, and tightened her arms around
her knees. She thought about asking the Elf once
more if he was in pain but knew that was futile. Of
course he was. There was nothing either of them
could do about it.

"Are you cold?" said the Elf.

"No," Marnie replied. She rested her cheek on
her knees, looking away from him. More silence.
She was lying, and knew he knew it. She was very
aware of the single blanket over her lap and his legs.

She wasn't going to take it from him. He needed it more.

They stayed silent awhile longer.

Finally the Elf said, "I take it the bucket over there is the, er, sanitary facilities?"

Marnie couldn't help it; she sniffed herself discreetly again, wondering how bad she and Yertle smelled. But she still couldn't tell. "Yes, that's it," she spat out. She wondered hysterically: should she apologize? No, it wasn't her fault—

"This is awkward," said the Elf calmly. "But I need . . . that is, I'm going to need help getting over there. Or maybe you could just bring it closer."

Marnie was consumed with the certain knowledge that she was an idiot. Not to mention selfish, unthinking . . . "Yes, of course," she managed. "Uh, which—which would you prefer?"

"Bring it closer," said the Elf. "And then if you could just help me stand . . ."

"Sure," said Marnie hastily. "Sure."

Marnie had no idea, during the whole little business that followed, if the Elf looked at her at all. She avoided looking at him. She had not known there was this much awkwardness and embarrassment in all the world. And she was aware, peripherally, that he wasn't quite as embarrassed as she was. Or maybe not even much at all. Somehow, that made things worse. Then, when she realized she needed to pee as well, and the Elf turned his back without her saying anything—and there was something so kind about it—abruptly, Marnie just wanted to kill him. Even though she knew that her anger wasn't about him at all, but about her, and all the things she was still trying to take in, to understand.

And now the Elf was apologizing, saying it was no big deal, and he was grateful for her help, using a gentle voice as if she was in nursery school. "Just shut up," Marnie said.

He did, but only for a few minutes. Then: "Is there any more seltzer?"

Marnie's throat closed up on her as that worry resurfaced. "Yes," she said. She got the bottle and handed it to him as he lay on the cot.

But he didn't take a drink. Instead he looked at the level of liquid and then tilted his head toward her. "That's all that's left?" he said.

Marnie settled herself again at the foot of the cot. She said carefully, "Until Leah comes back with more." *Or Max finds us. Or we die.*

"I see," said the Elf. He handed the bottle back to Marnie.

Marnie bit her lip. "You should have a small sip anyway, if you're thirsty."

"I'm not," said the Elf with forced nonchalance. "Why don't you go ahead?"

"Maybe later," said Marnie. She wrapped her arms around her legs again. The Elf closed his eyes and lay very still. Was he asleep, or only resting? Marnie couldn't tell. She watched him. She watched him, and time ticked past. It seemed like a very long time, and Leah Slaight didn't come, and Max didn't burst in with the cavalry, and eventually Marnie, too, closed her eyes, and finally, *finally*, let a stream of thoughts from the darkest part of herself flood into her head.

Leah Slaight had been unstable already; what dangerous gobbledygook would be going on in her head now? Surely the Elf's arrival would push her completely over the edge. She'd decide that her best bet was to kill both Marnie and the Elf, bury them in a marsh, and catch the first plane to some tropical paradise. Or maybe, while Leah was insanely considering her options, the Elf's leg would go septic and he'd die, screaming horribly, while Marnie watched, and *then* Leah would kill Marnie, or, better idea, simply leave her alone to die in the basement of loneliness and starvation, or no, dehydration would of course get Marnie before starvation did—terrible dry, parched sensations, choke, choke, gasp, the Elf's body putrefying over on the cot while with her last ounce of strength Marnie painted a death message in blood on the wall . . . and Max would arrive . . . too late, too late . . .

Exhausted, Marnie slipped into nightmare.

Llewellyne gripped the hilt of her heavy sword in both hands, all her muscles ready. She watched the Rubble-Eater warily, attentively. Above her head she heard the hawk calling advice: *Its brain is located directly behind the eye. That's where you should aim.*

Llewellyne nodded tensely.

The Rubble-Eater's blind eye looked straight into Llewellyne's, and it was empty of everything. The beast lowered its head and charged.

Llewellyne leapt to the right and swung at the beast's back with the flat of her sword, connecting with bone-jarring solidity. The hawk screeched in disappointment, disapproval. *What are you doing?*

The eye, the eye! The Rubble-Eater roared, turning about, but Llewellyne's sword had not even dented the stonelike hide of its back. Llewellyne danced a step or two away and stood poised.

"Back off," said Llewellyne aloud to the beast. "I don't want to hurt you." She had not the least belief, however, that it could understand her. It was said the Rubble-Eater had no language save its own senseless rumbling. It knew only food and not-food and was full of wordless hate. You could not reason with the Rubble-Eater. Everyone knew it.

The hawk was reminding her of it right now.

The Rubble-Eater lowered its head and charged again. At the last second, Llewellyne simply pivoted away and heard the hawk screech as the Rubble-Eater hurtled cleanly past, back to the other side of the cave.

For the third time, the Rubble-Eater charged. And, this time, Llewellyne lifted her chin and positioned her sword.

CHAPTER 23

"Marnie! Marn, wake up!"

For a very long moment after opening her dazed eyes to find the Elf with his hand on her shoulder and his concerned face near hers, Marnie actually thought that—like Dorothy and Toto waking up in Oz—they had somehow been transported to a real Paliopolis. It seemed quite natural for the Elf to be there with her, not as a screen glyph, but for real. Dimly she wondered where the Rubble-Eater had gone, and then, with an abrupt sinking of her stomach, she recalled its frantic charge, and her own sword, lifted—Automatically, she groped for her invisible hatpin. . . .

Then, as full awareness and memory returned, the illusion cracked and Marnie blinked in bewilderment. She moaned, burying her face in her hands for an instant before looking up at the Elf. "Sorry," she croaked.

"You were whimpering," said the Elf. He was very close, frowning. His hand patted her shoulder awkwardly. "You had a bad dream. Well, no wonder."

Marnie shuddered. Not meaning to, she nonetheless mumbled, "The Rubble-Eater . . ."

"The Rubble-Eater?" The Elf's voice was incredulous, and—was he laughing, now, a little? "Marn, you're dreaming of imaginary monsters? This place isn't good enough for you?" The laughter was gentle, though, and Marnie found she didn't mind the teasing. Gradually her head cleared completely. She realized she was still sitting up on the cot, her back slumped against the wall. How long had she slept? Minutes, hours? She swallowed with difficulty; she could use a—

Oh. For a mad moment, Marnie imagined an entire supermarket row of plastic seltzer bottles with stick arms and legs, waving top hats and kicking together in a chorus line. Lemon-lime, white grape, mango, raspberry . . . No. She swallowed again, banishing the vision. She looked at the Elf, and then around the cold, dreary little basement room.

"Silly, huh?" she managed. She found herself looking down at the Elf's hand, large-knuckled and warm on her shoulder. He saw her looking and withdrew it, and she felt relieved and bereft at once.

Somehow he'd shifted himself on the cot, closer to her, sitting up on her end. Marnie found her gaze pulled to his thigh, where the strip of T-shirt was bound. Was that an angry red at the edge of the makeshift bandage? Marnie glanced at the Elf's face, where the laughter had faded, and she bit back the

147

inevitable question about how he was feeling. "Did you sleep?" she asked instead.

He hesitated and then shrugged. "I went somewhere for a while. I don't know if it was sleep, exactly. Ever feel like . . . like you're awake but can't move? Can't open your eyes, can't shift your body? You're conscious, or you think you are, but you're not sure, because you might just be dreaming that you're awake. I'm not describing it well . . ."

Marnie *had* felt the way he was describing, and recently, too. Fear curdled in her. She recalled the weight of the Elf's hand on her shoulder . . . the warmth of it. She said abruptly, "I bet you have a fever. Let me feel your forehead." She shifted, rebalancing, and started to reach out.

The Elf recoiled as if she were Leah Slaight. "No, I'm okay." Marnie stared at him, the rebuff echoing inside her but not yet fully assimilated, and he stared back. Then, to her surprise, his eyes dropped. He said, "Okay, yeah, maybe I do have a fever. I feel kind of hot. It's okay, though. I'll be fine. Don't worry."

Slowly, of its own accord, Marnie's hand again stretched out, and this time he didn't back away. She placed the whole of her palm on the Elf's forehead. It was like a small oven. She frowned, and the Elf, warily, met her gaze. His eyes looked a little wild; Marnie imagined she could actually see the fever behind them. But she could see sanity there too, and stability. And a deep kind of sureness.

"I'll be fine," said the Elf again uncomfortably. He shook her hand off and hunched a shoulder.

Weird, Marnie thought. So weird that in real life—once you got past the bald head and camouflage outfit, that is—the thieving, laughing Elf should seem so . . . so steadfast. "You ought to lie down," she said.

Silently he obeyed. Marnie automatically shook the blanket out over him, but he grabbed it and thrust it back toward her. "You're the one who's cold. At least . . ." He hesitated and then propped himself up again on his elbows and looked at her— almost but not quite making eye contact. "I won't bite. At least let me share it." But when Marnie didn't respond, he threw the blanket at her, slumped back down, and turned away, onto his side.

Marnie didn't move for an entire minute. Or perhaps it was five minutes, or ten, or half an hour. During this time she had some odd thoughts, most of them completely unconnected. She thought about Max and Skye. About Skye, so full of love and so alone. About Jenna Lowry, crying and crying over whatever had happened with hockey boy. Then about Leah Slaight. She felt her fingers curl into tight fists on the blanket. She imagined stabbing Leah, again and again and again and again. . . .

At last, having made no decision that she could name or understand, Marnie found herself shifting to lie down on the cot, on her side, against the Elf's back. She quickly realized that there was no sense trying to keep an inch or two between them. The cot was narrow, the Elf weighed more than Marnie, and she slid right up against him. Well, so be it. She got the blanket over both of them and settled uneasily against his hot back, one arm beneath her head, the other awkward at her side.

She closed her eyes and stayed as still as she could. She heard her own breath; it sounded anxious, wheezy. She tried—unsuccessfully—to banish her awareness of the last time she'd been this close to anyone. It had been Skye, of course. Five years, nearly six, since that last hug from Skye, before she boarded her airplane and disappeared forever. The last hug, ever.

The Elf was a furnace, and, after a time, Marnie began to feel warm. Then, miserably, helplessly, she found herself wondering again whether she smelled. She hated herself for it. He was sick with fever, and she was worried about whether he found her repulsive! Talk about insignificant . . . talk about self-obsessed . . . what was wrong with her, what?

The Elf was lying very still as well. Marnie would have thought he was asleep, except that she knew he wasn't. Then he reached back lightly. Marnie felt herself tense up even more as his hand found her arm and then ran down the length of her forearm to her wrist. She felt the brush of his fingers over her pulse, her palm. Then they entwined with hers, and his hand gripped tight. Too tight, for a moment. But then . . . just there. Gripping. Solid.

Something deep within Marnie hesitated but then—relaxed. Her fingers moved in the Elf's grasp. And then gripped back, hard. In the time that followed, they were quiet—not asleep, not moving.

Marnie, for once, did no thinking at all. Instead, with her whole body, she felt what it was like to have allowed another human being near.

CHAPTER 24

Marnie thought it was perhaps an hour later, though she knew her sense of time was completely messed up. But all at once the Elf stirred and mumbled, hoarsely, "I've lost my mind." He scrambled frantically off the cot, landing on his knees and levering himself to a standing position. He reeled as soon as he was upright, but then regained his balance and, by what seemed like sheer will, traversed the room in a staggering half-run. He grabbed the knob of the door and yanked.

Marnie sat up. "It's locked, Elf. I checked."

He ignored her. His breath sounded choppy. He was staring at the door, at the frame. He wavered again and leaned one hand against the door to support himself while, head thrown slightly back, he kept on staring. "It opens out," he said.

"I know," said Marnie patiently. "If it opened in, I'd have pulled out the hinge pins."

"Gonna break it down," said the Elf. "I'm *stupid*. 'S only wood, right? I can do it." He let go of the door, staggered backward, and threw himself against it. It thudded and tossed him back. Marnie felt her body jerk as it had when she'd been on the other side of that very door, with Leah shoving. Leah had made headway then, but the door hadn't been locked with that sturdy padlock on the other side. Still, the Elf was heavy . . . maybe . . . She jumped up and managed to catch him just as he bounced off the door a second time. She nearly fell with him.

"Cops do this all the time," panted the Elf.

Under the shortened T-shirt, Marnie's arm was right against his skin. He was, if anything, hotter than before. Cops had training, she thought; cops used their legs. Cops were probably athletic, and somehow she doubted that the Elf spent much time at a gym. She thought of the poor Rubble-Eater. "It's thick wood," she heard herself saying. "A heavy lock. I don't want you to get hurt—"

"What's *wrong* with you?" snarled the Elf. "You wanna stay here?" His bald head gleamed in the harsh light of the overhead bulb. He wrested himself away from her and landed against the door again—with less force than before. He slumped and clung to the door frame. "You're useless!" he hissed over his shoulder.

Marnie's teeth clamped together. Useless! She'd had a perfectly good escape attempt under way earlier—far better, far more intelligent than the Elf's strongarm tactics—and *he* had ruined it. "Fine," she said between her teeth. "We can *both* throw ourselves against the door." She thought again of the Rubble-Eater.

"Good," mumbled the Elf. The fingers of one of his hands peeled off the door frame, and Marnie stepped close to grab him before he fell.

"Just don't blame me," said Marnie, helping him take a step or two back, "if all the racket brings Leah down here with her gun."

"Hope it *does*. One . . . two . . ."

They both threw themselves against the door. The impact of their combined weight was considerably less than Marnie would have imagined. She could feel the downward drag of the Elf's body in her arms; downward, not forward. He was wheezing now. In her inner ear, she could hear the Sorceress laughing sourly.

"Again," said the Elf between his teeth.

"Maybe if we rested first and then—"

"We don't know how much time we *have*!" The Elf tore himself free from Marnie and landed against the door once more. This time it barely thudded and he fell, twisting on the bad ankle. A grunt escaped him. Of pain? Anger? All at once there was something, too, about the look of his neck. How could the nape of a neck look so vulnerable, so defeated?

Before she could think, Marnie had her arm around his shoulders. "Get up," she said. "We'll try it together again. Even if we can't break it down now, we can—we can weaken it for later."

He shot her an incredulous look, but got willingly to his feet. For the first time Marnie felt his full weight on her shoulders and understood he

154

hadn't really been leaning on her before. She swallowed. Somewhere in the back of her mind, she registered how very, very dry her throat was. "Come on," she said to the Elf. She knew now for sure that this was not going to work; they were not going to break the door down. But it didn't matter.

They threw themselves against it several more times. With each attempt, the amount of force lessened. Impossibly, the door seemed to have gotten stronger. Marnie knew she wouldn't stop until the Elf said to—and that this wouldn't happen until he could not get up off the floor, even with her help.

When he finally did collapse, on his knees in front of the impervious door, Marnie—panting, on her knees herself—found she had to turn away, so that she wouldn't see how his shoulders looked, hunched in defeat.

He surprised her, though, by talking again. "We had to try," he said, somewhat uncertainly.

Marnie nodded. She looked over at him; his back was to her. She said creakily, "Yes." Her eyes wandered across the room to the seltzer bottle. She couldn't see the level of liquid clearly. She licked her dry lips. "Elf? Would you like a drink?"

Silence. She knew he had heard her. Finally he said, his voice as creaky as hers: "Okay. Maybe a little one." A pause that went on a bit long. Marnie knew he didn't have the strength to move yet. "In a minute," he said eventually.

Marnie didn't feel much like moving either. The seltzer bottle was a few feet away, near the cot. She could crawl there. She thought about that for a while and then suddenly realized she had done it.

She was on her hands and knees next to the cot, reaching out for the bottle. Grasping it. She collapsed back onto her heels—realizing vaguely that her feet hurt; she'd scraped them even more raw on the cement floor, and her tights were in pieces around her ankles. She squinted at the bottle, at the water level.

Maybe two inches of seltzer left.

"It's not much." The Elf was at her elbow. Marnie turned her head; her eyes were almost level with his. He'd crawled too. His forehead was damp with sweat. Were his eyes looking a little clearer, though? His voice was a mere thread.

Feed a cold; starve a fever. Or was it the other way around? Either way, you were supposed to drink. Her fingers were trembling. She uncapped the bottle and held it out to him.

He didn't move his eyes from hers. "You first."

"Oh, no." The word got trapped in her throat. She had to try again. "No. You."

After a long moment, the Elf took the bottle and held it up, examining, like Marnie, the level. Still looking at it, not drinking, he said to Marnie, "It's been a full day since she left us here."

"No!" said Marnie. "It's been a few hours."

The Elf held out his wrist. There was a watch on it. Marnie wondered how she had missed noticing it before. It was the kind with a day and date as well as the time. She blinked in shock. Then she looked up.

The Elf rested the bottle on the floor, as if, even near empty, it was too heavy to hold. "How long between her visits before?"

Marnie knew where he was going. "I don't know

for sure. I wasn't feeling very well some of the time." Her hand drifted up to the still-tender lump on her head. Noticing that the Elf's eyes had followed the movement, she pulled her hand away and added quickly, "I think she probably checked in once a day."

The Elf was looking grim. And tired, and a little crazed. Then his face smoothed out again, became blank. "Do you honestly think she's coming back?" he asked.

Marnie found that her eyes had fixed on the seltzer bottle. She couldn't drag them away. She watched the Elf's hands as he lifted it again. All at once the bottle's mouth was against her cheek. Her lips. She thought his hands were shaking slightly.

She turned her face away. "No."

"Just a sip," he said, still in that rasp.

The bottle was against her face. Its mouth against hers—

"No!" Marnie snarled. She grabbed the bottle, not caring that it meant grabbing his hand as well, and started to push. "Put it away!"

Somehow his other hand was over hers, on the bottle, stilling their battle. He said, "She knows it's all the water we have, doesn't she?" When Marnie didn't answer, he said it again: "Doesn't she?"

Marnie found she couldn't actually say yes. "She's crazy. Maybe she forgot."

He sighed. "Have a small sip. Please, Marn. Go on. Good. Good girl."

I'll good-girl you, Marnie thought. She let the few drops of flat seltzer linger in her mouth as long as she could. Then she allowed them to trickle down her throat. She closed her eyes for a second. She had never appreciated how wonderfully *wet* liquid could be.

He was still holding the bottle near her. She pushed it away, and this time he let her. She watched him hesitate, then take a small sip as well. Then he twisted the cap back on and put the bottle down.

"How much did you pour over my stupid leg?" he said.

"As little as I could," said Marnie quietly, and watched him nod.

After a while, she helped him back to the cot. He needed to lean fully on her to get there. She had hoped the sweat meant his fever was breaking, but his skin felt as hot as before. Most worrisome of all, after a few minutes she asked him to take another small sip of the seltzer . . . and he did.

CHAPTER 25

Weird how she wasn't embarrassed anymore. Worry and fear—and, yes, the tight tentacles of a ferociously controlled panic—had pushed that emotion right out. It seemed almost natural when the Elf automatically shifted over on the narrow cot, nearer the wall, to make room for Marnie. She hesitated only because she thought she should look at the bullet wound again first.

"Why?" said the Elf. "There isn't anything more you can do."

Marnie blinked. True, but . . . "I'd like to know," she said. "Wouldn't you?"

"No," said the Elf. His hand clamped over the bandage as if to protect it from her.

She gave in. She moved to lie down, this time with her back to him. She could feel his breathing, harsh in the stillness. She guessed his eyes were shut. She guessed he was in pain. Her own body was

159

beginning to ache from the attack on the door. It would be worse tomorrow, and even worse the day after that. Assuming they were still here. Assuming they were still alive . . .

How long, Marnie wondered morbidly, did it take to die of dehydration? "Hey," she said. "You okay, Elf?"

"Yeah."

Silence again. The room rang with it. Marnie felt she couldn't endure it. "Talk to me," she said desperately to the Elf. "Talk about anything. School, your parents, your family. Your friend David. Anything. Just—Just talk." She flexed her right hand. It felt empty. She wished he had reached to hold it again. She knew she couldn't reach for his. She just couldn't.

"Maybe later," said the Elf after another moment. Oh, God, Marnie thought. She was a selfish fool. Asking him to talk! Was his voice hoarser now? Should she make him drink again? There wasn't much left, but . . .

"You talk to me," said the Elf. And then: "Please."

"Oh," said Marnie. Her mind went blank. Beneath that, new panic bubbled. She knew what he wanted.

"You were going to tell me . . ." He paused for breath. ". . . a long story. Your side of how this happened. Remember?"

Marnie thought about talking, about telling him how—at least in part. And why. And as she thought, she breathed more and more shallowly. Where would she begin? What parts could she say;

what should she leave out? Who was the Elf to her, to hear anything? To ask anything? She didn't know him! She wasn't the hired entertainment! Stories to die by . . . no, *no* . . .

"Or," the Elf said, "don't tell me anything."

Oh, God. She'd hurt his feelings. But—

"Don't you try to guilt-trip me," she snapped.

She actually felt his whole body go rigid with anger. He said nothing for a full minute. When he did speak, the words came out in a rush, as if he'd spent the time building up enough strength to get it all out.

"I'm part of this! You didn't ask me to be, but I am. Deal with it! Grow up! This isn't virtual reality. You're not the high-scoring player! And I deserve to know what's going on."

Marnie reached for her own rage, but it had dissolved. He was right. She knew he was. What had made her angry, anyway? She couldn't remember. She put her face in her hands. She took a deep breath, and then another.

She just didn't think she could talk.

"You okay?" the Elf said. He sounded tired, so tired.

Tired of her, probably. Marnie couldn't help that. She took another breath. She felt the cot move; the Elf was shifting, laboriously getting up on one elbow to look down at her.

"Okay," he said after a moment. "It's all right. Nobody's going to make you. Ve do not haf vays . . . Look, never mind. Marn. You don't have to. If it's too difficult. I—I just want to help."

Marnie didn't remove her hands from her face.

161

"Don't talk to me like I'm a mental patient," she whispered.

Silence. Then: "I'm not. How do you want me to talk to you?"

The trouble was, she didn't know. She didn't know. Like a friend? What was that? How was that? She didn't know. *He* had a friend, this Dave. His buddy, he'd said. That was a stupid word, buddy. Buddy buddy buddy. Rhymed with bloody . . .

That crazy woman thought she was Skye's daughter. Marnie's sister. She really thought it. What if the Elf didn't understand why the very idea made Marnie so frightened?

I deserve to know what's going on, he had said.

"You've been here five days," said the Elf after a while. He was still looking at her; Marnie could feel it. "It's a long time."

Marnie felt her head move in a nod. She wanted to raise her head. She wanted to look at the Elf. But she just couldn't.

She was burningly thirsty again. She wondered, idly, if you could drink tears, or if, like seawater, they would make you all the thirstier. Now was not the time to find out. She suspected tears accelerated dehydration.

The Elf's life was at stake here too. His and hers. Two lives involved in this ludicrous mess.

Three, corrected the Sorceress-voice unexpectedly. *Be accurate. Leah Slaight is a living person.*

Two, Marnie repeated to herself firmly. Only two, Me and the Elf.

The Sorceress was silent. Marnie removed her

hands—and nearly recoiled off the cot. The Elf's face was almost touching hers. He was leaning over her, frowning. For a moment she actually thought he was going to stroke her cheek. Reflexively she moved away a trace. He didn't touch her. She was glad, glad.

"Crying?" asked the Elf.

"No," said Marnie defiantly, but the Sorceress-voice was suddenly screeching at her. *I am so tired of you, Marnie! You and your cowardly ways—*

Shut up, Marnie thought. You—you icon. You're nothing without me.

I am you, you drooling nitwit.

No, thought Marnie. No. Wrong. Wrong.

Skye would want you to be strong. . . .

I don't care. I hate Skye! Marnie thought suddenly. I hate her for leaving me.

The Sorceress did not reply.

The Elf was saying something, but Marnie wasn't sure what it was. It took her a moment to find her voice. "I'm sorry," she said then. "I didn't hear you. I was . . . thinking." She chanced a look up at the Elf. He was sweating again. He was sick.

And she, Marnie Skyedottir, was an ass.

"Are you all right?" she said. It was a stupid thing to say, but there was nothing else.

Predictably, the Elf nodded tightly. "Yeah." But when Marnie turned and reached out to help him ease back down on the cot, he let her. And then he closed his eyes, for a long moment.

She discovered that she had made up her mind. She heard herself say, "You're right. I'll tell you everything, okay? And . . . And I—I apologize. You do deserve to know."

"Apology accepted," said the Elf without opening his eyes. He flung one arm over his forehead. "Talk. I'll listen."

CHAPTER 26

I t felt to Marnie as if she talked forever. With her eyes closed, the blanket over her, her hands under her cheek, and the Elf breathing quietly yet audibly behind her, it was not unlike being in some hypnotic state. Dreamily, her voice barely louder than a whisper, she told the Elf everything she could articulate, without even trying to figure out what was and wasn't important. The Elf didn't ask questions or prompt or try to interpret or say anything at all beyond the occasional "yeah" or "uh-huh" whenever Marnie paused to say, "Does that make any sense at all?" or "Do you know what I mean?" Yet she knew he was listening, listening hard; she could feel his attention, sense his focus on her words, even—she imagined—sense him thinking.

She began by talking about being at the Halsett Grille with Leah Slaight but soon felt compelled to backtrack into her history with Leah. The Elf let out a snort of laughter when she related the covalent bonds/Matthew 5:39 episode. Then, as she told about the meeting with the dean and Mrs. Fisher, she could feel him tense and for a second she thought he would speak. But he didn't.

He listened.

At first Marnie found it distinctly odd to speak at length like this, out loud, without having her words guided by—or, more likely, meant to defend against—someone else's desires or expectations. She couldn't help suspecting that if the Elf had been feeling better, he would have interrupted more. He was no saint of patience, and once or twice when she headed off on an apparent tangent, she could actually feel him move to speak and then stop. In the back of her mind, she found this amusing, even a little endearing. In his place, she thought, she'd never have been able to stay quiet.

If this was in fact what listening was, she knew no one had ever listened to her before in her life. Her stomach twisted and she felt her stream of words stumble for a moment before she gathered herself again.

She found herself helplessly diverting into tales of her history at Halsett, and then at the other boarding school, and from there to Max, and from there, of course, to Skye.

Skye. Back and back and back and back to Skye. Somehow, every branch of the story seemed finally to leave Marnie with Skye's name on her lips. Marnie would hesitate, then jump away to another branch after speaking only the minimum, only what was necessary, only the facts. She'd firmly reconnect to the main thread of her story, only to wander off again on some byroad and there once more be confronted, inevitably, with Skye.

The third or fourth time this happened, she suddenly realized that she had circled and circled but had yet to speak of the days when she'd been imprisoned alone in this place. Or rather, of the talks, if they could be called that, with Leah. Instead she dwelled overlong on her development of the strategic plan to explode the seltzer bottle. She thought then, What am I doing? She fell silent.

The Elf said, "Seltzer?"

Marnie nodded automatically.

"I'd like some," the Elf clarified, and Marnie sat up and reached for the bottle. She noted the water level. She watched the Elf prop himself up—was it her imagination or did he look less flushed?—and take a sip. A tiny sip. Still, it seemed somehow wrong to refuse again when he handed the open bottle to her. She upended it and allowed a small amount into her mouth. She let it rest there for a very long time before she swallowed. She wondered why she wasn't hungry at all; and then wondered if the Elf was. She asked him, knowing that he'd say no. He did.

He said calmly, as if he could read her mind through all the surface-level chatter: "Okay. The thing you're avoiding. Are you gonna tell me?"

He sounded better, Marnie thought. And she found she couldn't lie, couldn't evade, anymore. He deserved to know. She looked back at him, straight into those incredibly beautiful Elf eyes. She said, low: "She thinks—Leah thinks—she says—she's my sister. Half sister. Skye's daughter."

It was like a cork exploding from a champagne bottle. After it came streams and streams of words, tumbling from her mouth.

There's no way—just no way—but I couldn't help doing the math, figuring out how old Skye would've been . . . and it's not impossible—but I don't believe it . . . but there's so much, you see, that I don't know about her. About Skye, I mean. I don't even know her real name!

Maybe she didn't mean to keep secrets from me, it's that I was so little—

My father—my biological father—I don't want to know—I really don't, it doesn't matter, but sometimes—I can't help wondering—nothing to do with this, I know . . .

Leah Slaight's a madwoman, she really, really is, I keep coming back to that, I know that's true, but—but—what if . . . ?

And this kidnapping; you asked why Max couldn't figure it out . . . it's because he doesn't know a thing about me, not really, I don't let him, he's tried but I don't let him . . . it's my fault that he'd think I might run away, do something stupid . . . My fault we're going to die.

I'm sorry, I'm so very, very sorry—what the hell were you doing online anyway, Elf, you're one of the good kids, aren't you? I can tell; good grades, going to a good college, I bet—wait, it'll be April fifteen soon, right? That means college acceptances will come . . . I bet ten thousand of them will be waiting at home for

168

you. My fault—I'm so sorry, Elf. I didn't even ask, don't you have a family . . . bet they're worried . . . bet they're sitting with all the college letters, out of their minds with worry—hey, why haven't they come looking for you, didn't you tell them where you were going? Oh, Elf, I'm sorry . . .

Later, Marnie never knew with certainty what she'd said aloud and what she hadn't, or the degree to which any of it was coherent. She didn't know when she started crying like a fool, nor when it was that the Elf grabbed her and held her so that she ended up babbling and sobbing and snuffling into the shoulder of his camouflage T-shirt. "Hey," he kept saying soothingly. "Hey."

As she calmed, Marnie had an abrupt memory of herself holding Jenna Lowry in a way that was not unlike this. Marnie had said, It's okay, to Jenna then. Without knowing a damned thing, she had said that. No wonder Jenna had been angry, Marnie thought now. No wonder. In fact, Marnie was lucky Jenna hadn't slugged her.

The Elf did not say, It's okay. He just kept on with the heys. Another few weeks, Marnie thought, full of self-loathing, and who knew, he might even have had a Paliopolis score that was higher than hers. He did way better on human interaction, that was for sure.

She realized after a time that she was hideously uncomfortable; that she was crouched on the cot with one leg nearly numb beneath her; that she needed desperately to blow her nose. And—incredibly, because she'd drunk so little—to use Yertle.

The Elf kept saying, Hey. He was so warm. She

169

liked having him stroke her bristly hair. She liked
the way his arms felt. She liked him, so much.

And, she suddenly realized, she'd never bothered
to ask him one single thing about himself. What
music he listened to. What he wanted to study in
college. What his family was like. What he and his
friends did when they hung out. Oh my God, she
thought. She didn't even know his real—

The Sorceress in her head interrupted snidely.
Oh, please get off it. This isn't a date!

Which was true.

He was so warm. She wondered what would happen if she turned in his arms and hugged him back.
If she tipped up her head and—

No! You stink, remember?

Marnie cringed. She took a deep breath, muttered, "Sorry. Thanks," pushed away from the Elf,
and, gulping in more air, turned her back on him.
Surreptitiously she wiped her nose on her sleeve.

She could feel him behind her. But she wouldn't
turn and look. She wouldn't say anything. She
didn't dare. She'd got him shot. His leg was probably screaming in pain. She was now on the point of
getting him killed. And . . . and she *smelled*.

After another minute, chin held high, forcing her
numb leg to work, she managed to make her way
over to Yertle.

CHAPTER
27

Marnie didn't look at the Elf, but she knew he was doing the polite thing, back turned and all that. She was so full of uncertainty about what she should say now, to make it very clear that she was back in control of herself and didn't need help or pity or . . . or anything, that the Elf surprised her by simply speaking. "Marnie, I'm terrified too. As if you couldn't guess. But I thought it should be said."

Mr. Macho Cyberspace Hero thought it was important to say he was scared? Marnie blinked and suppressed the stupid impulse to deny that *she* was frightened. A secret bit of her was relieved that he thought that was why she'd turned away from him. "Okay," she said uncertainly. She got up cautiously from her squat. She stayed where she was, across the room from the Elf. She watched his back as he spoke.

He said, "I have a few things to say, okay?" And after the barest of pauses, he continued. "Point one: I'd really rather not die. I'm not ready to give up. We haven't fully tried thinking our way through this yet. There might be something we haven't realized. Some way out."

Marnie knew this cell better than the Elf. She'd explored it before he came. If Leah really had abandoned them, if Max didn't somehow see past all the red herrings Marnie had unthinkingly piled in the way, they were dead. "You sound a little better," she temporized.

"Yeah, yeah," said the Elf. "I feel a little less woozy than I did before. My head's clearer." He hesitated. "You done over there?"

"Yes," Marnie said.

The Elf turned. There was a focused, determined look on his face. "Come back and sit down, so I can look at you while we talk?"

After a moment, Marnie sat. There was no sensible reason to refuse.

"I know you're pessimistic that Leah will come back," the Elf was saying. "And now that you've told me about this sister thing I understand why." He hesitated and then added, "But what I'm thinking is, if she's truly crazy, then she might still come. You know? Sure, it's logical for her to abandon us, hope we die or whatever—but maybe she's not logical." He leaned toward Marnie. "Is that possible?"

"Maybe," said Marnie doubtfully.

"You think she won't be back." A statement, not a question.

"I think we're going to die here," said Marnie bluntly.

"I know, but—" The Elf stopped and sighed. He put one hand up to his head, and Marnie noticed that he had dark stubble. She'd read somewhere that hair and nail cells still grew after death. Maybe by the time their bodies were found, the Elf would have a full head of hair. His family wouldn't recognize him.

"It's just not productive to think that way," said the Elf.

He wanted productive thinking? "Well, by all means," Marnie snapped. "Let's banish all negative thoughts. Come on. Let's throw ourselves at the door again, so we'll feel like we're doing something. Or do you have a better idea this time, Elf? Something more *productive*?"

Marnie stared defiantly at the Elf, whose jaw had dropped.

Then, unexpectedly, he grinned. "You drive me up the wall. You always have, even in Paliopolis. Look." He stopped and then said, in an oddly tentative voice, "Marn . . . do you think you could try remembering for more than five minutes that I'm on your side?"

I can't afford that! Marnie thought uncontrollably. Then she was appalled at herself. Where had that come from? Why? When she knew that here, now, they were a team . . .

She turned her face away. Eventually she said flatly, "I know that. I'm sorry. I just . . . you must think I'm nuts."

He was quiet for so long that she figured he was trying to find a way to say yes. A nice way, of course, because the Elf was a nice guy. A nice, normal teenage guy with a family and buddies and good grades and college plans and everything. Probably he had a girlfriend, too, and he was looking at Marnie and wishing he were safely with her. She wanted to throw up.

He said, "I think you're scared. I think this is terrifying, probably more terrifying for you than I can imagine. And I think . . ."

Marnie couldn't stand it. "What?"

"I think you're really used to being alone."

It was like a stab in the throat.

She tried to think of something to say. She wondered why it was so awful, hearing something aloud, from someone else, when you'd said it to yourself a million times. When you knew, yourself . . .

The Elf said, "I know what that's about. Believe me, I do."

Marnie made a shrugging movement.

"Look at me, Marn," the Elf said. He sounded kind of impatient.

Marnie took in a little puff of breath. She set her mouth in a straight, firm, tight line. She turned back. She tried to say, "What?" but the word only formed on her lips and didn't quite make it out into the air.

The Elf said, "Do I *look* like Mr. Popularity?"

Finally Marnie managed to say something. "You have friends. This buddy Dave guy."

"I have *a* friend," corrected the Elf. "And he's

marginal too, in his own way." He paused and then added, "Don't get the wrong idea. I don't have a problem with that. And it's not as if I go around collecting losers. I just—I kind of like people who . . ." He paused. "People who are a little different." He looked directly at Marnie. "You're a little different. I like that. Do you believe me?"

She thought about it and found that she didn't. She couldn't. She shrugged again.

"Don't you like yourself?" demanded the Elf.

Marnie stared at him. It was not a question that had ever occurred to her. She knew that no one—except Skye—had ever liked her.

Of course, you've never let anyone close enough to find out, whispered the Sorceress.

It was as if the Elf read her mind. "I didn't ask about whether other people liked you. I asked if you liked yourself."

Marnie's mouth twisted. "Yes," she said. "I mean, I'm not perfect, but . . . yeah." Her voice strengthened. "Yeah. I like myself. I believe in myself. I don't care that I'm not the same as everyone else."

The Elf nodded. "What I actually believe is that everybody is truly strange, unique, if you look closely. But most people are desperate to hide it. Desperate to blend in, to not be noticed. So they play all these games . . . do what they think other people want them to do and say what they think other people want them to say; don't even dare *feel* what they really feel. Especially kids our age, you know? God forbid anybody should stick out. You

175

know what I'm saying?" The Elf's stubbled head bobbed with intensity.

Almost against her will, Marnie found herself drawn into what the Elf was saying. He was so passionate. She felt as if she were listening to some kind of manifesto. The Elf philosophy. And he wasn't wrong. Marnie thought of Jenna Lowry and her gaggle of friends. And then of Jenna—a different Jenna—crying. She wondered, unexpectedly, if Jenna felt misunderstood by her friends. If she ever felt alone . . .

"Yeah," she said, and heard with surprise that her voice had strength again. "I know what you're saying."

"I'm not interested in blending in," continued the Elf, "and I decided a long time ago that I wouldn't even try, no matter what it cost." His expression had gone a little defiant. A little proud. A little—shy? Vulnerable? No, that couldn't be.

"And you," said the Elf. "You don't try to blend in either, Marn. Even online, you stuck out. In person . . ." He made a vague hand motion, and Marnie found her own hand at her cheek. She thought of her makeup, her hair. Blend in? Fat chance.

"I think maybe my reasons were—are—different from yours," she said.

The Elf leaned forward. "A lot different?"

It was suddenly easy to share. "There was never any hope of my blending in," Marnie said simply. "Skye, you know. Once I figured that out, I went the other way. Flaunted it. It just seemed like the thing to do."

Looking thoughtful, the Elf nodded. "I can see that." Then he said abruptly, "Did you know you're one of the most popular topics of discussion in the Paliopolis chat rooms? Nobody could figure you out, but they loved trying. Did you ever lurk and listen? Under another name, maybe?"

Marnie stared.

"I guess not," said the Elf. "You were always playing. Even the Dungeon Master said he didn't have a clue who you were. And you never chatted with anyone. It was always business with you. It was always the game."

Marnie's mind was spinning. Other people weren't in Paliopolis for the game alone? That was the stupidest thing she'd ever heard! They went there to *chat*? About *what*? They didn't know each other! And what were they doing talking about *her*? And the Elf . . .

Finally Marnie said slowly, "You don't seem like a gamer to me, Elf. You did in Paliopolis, of course. But in person . . . something's just not right."

"I was doing research," said the Elf. "On online communities. Paliopolis was just one of them."

"But—you were playing. And you're not bad . . . you were actually getting frighteningly good. And you spent a lot of time there this spring. . . ."

"I got interested," said the Elf. All at once he blushed. Fiercely. And Marnie couldn't help it: she thought of the fifteen e-mails she would never read. She looked away. Toward the door.

And then, *at* the door.

And at the door frame.

At the way the door fit—or rather, was currently *not* fitting—in the door frame.

The Elf was talking. Marnie reached behind her and seized his arm. Hard.

"Hey!" he said. "Marn—"

Her hand tightened, and she cut her eyes toward him. "Shhh!" she mouthed. With her other hand, she pointed. The Elf stilled as he saw what she did. They had not broken the door, but nevertheless—

It was an inch ajar.

Someone had opened it.

CHAPTER 28

The Elf's eyes nearly bugged out of his head. Recovering, he mouthed, "Is someone out there?" and Marnie moved her free hand in an I-don't-know gesture. She supposed, however, that Leah was eavesdropping—most likely accompanied by her gun. She could tell that this was what the Elf thought as well. Together they mouthed, "Leah?"

The air suddenly pulsed with renewed possibilities. And, of course, with immediate danger. Abruptly Marnie felt her heart rate triple. She pulled breath deeply into her lungs. This is it, she thought. The location of the door, and the angle of the opening, meant whoever was out there could not see them. Could not see the cot at all. Could only hear.

This was their chance. Maybe their only chance.

Marnie said aloud, in a voice that sounded nearly normal, "So, what made you interested in researching online communities?" and saw that for a split second the Elf thought she had finally snapped under the pressure. But then his lashes flickered in comprehension, and he began babbling rather fluently about advanced placement psychology. Marnie couldn't help wasting a moment on the reflection that it figured: She got treated like a criminal for hanging out online, while the Elf called it independent study and got academic credit.

The Elf was frowning a question at Marnie, and she shrugged. It didn't need saying. The Elf was disabled. If anybody was going to tiptoe over to the door, slam it fully open, and do . . . well, whatever next seemed to be the thing to do—it would have to be Marnie. She gestured, *You stay here!* to the Elf and let go of his arm, only then becoming aware that she'd been clutching it the way a child clutches a doll in the dark. She hoped she hadn't hurt him. She further hoped that between now and the door, inspiration would strike. She eased quietly to her feet—

—And the Elf grabbed her arm, arresting her. "Amazingly, it turns out there are interesting parallels between sites that are organized around chat and gaming communities like Paliopolis," he expounded wildly. As Marnie turned an incredulous face on him—had he lost it?—he used her for partial leverage to struggle to his feet beside her, all the while continuing to speak.

Then, entirely predictably, he staggered. Marnie used the moment to let him know in no uncertain terms—it was amazing how much you could say in silence, by scowling and baring your teeth—that he would only get in the way. In *her* way. He snarled right back, flailing his left hand to indicate that nothing and no one was keeping him in this room. Marnie wished ferociously that this was Paliopolis and she could bespell him to freeze where he stood. Or better yet, club him over the head.

They were wasting time. She mouthed, "Trust me, you idiot," wrenched herself free of him, and launched into a silent, rapid stalk toward the door. Just short of it, she reached out without thinking and grabbed up Yertle by its handle, moving it into position before her. As she did so she heard the Elf's prattle falter for a second before continuing: ". . . irrepressible social bonding instinct of nearly all humans in any circumstances . . ."

She had no idea if he was following her. She hoped he wasn't. She wished at the very least she had watched more kung fu movies.

She kicked the door hard, with her left foot. It slammed open.

And bounced back. Marnie caught it with her foot before it slammed shut.

There was no other sound. No gasp or hiss from Leah. No crack of wild, spontaneous gunfire. No sound to indicate the direction in which Marnie should aim the contents of the bucket.

Nothing.

Perplexed, Marnie glanced over her shoulder at the Elf. He'd made it halfway across the room. She saw him shrug at the same moment that she felt her own shoulders move identically.

She swiveled her head back, listening hard to the ringing emptiness, and took three seconds to think.

181

It was probably already too late. Leah was probably out there, holding her gun, aiming it at the door. If Marnie stepped through it . . . But they couldn't stay here. Her plan . . . well. She clutched Yertle. Her plan was to face Leah and win. Somehow.

Marnie kicked the door again and raced through as it slammed open. But at the moment she crossed the threshold, she knew. The skin stretching over her entire body stood at attention and told her. She stopped dead. She stood still and looked around, as if to confirm what she was already certain of.

"Elf," she said after a moment. She spoke in a whisper, but knew her voice was clear enough to be heard. "Elf, she's not out here."

The Elf had already hobbled to the doorway. Marnie cast one last disbelieving look around before putting down Yertle and going to assist him. He shrugged off her hand, however, and leaned against the wall. He too scanned the room in puzzled astonishment. "What the . . . ?"

"Leah opened it and left?" Marnie asked dubiously. But it seemed the only possible explanation. The door had been firmly locked. Had she come to her senses? Were they expected to leave quietly?

Or was Leah waiting at the top of the stairs with her gun? Marnie could think of no earthly reason why she would do that . . . but . . .

The Elf said hoarsely, "Marn, I have no clue anymore. Is she letting us go?"

Marnie's eyes wandered to the stairs and then back to the Elf.

He too was now looking thoughtfully at the stairs. Then he surveyed the room, his eyes stopping on the pile of two-by-fours. "I guess it's time for us to split up," he said. "You have to be the one to go upstairs."

"Yeah," said Marnie. She had come to the same conclusion. It was the logical way to proceed. Still, she blinked once, hard, and then felt her whole body shudder.

"You want a piece of wood?" said the Elf, nodding at the two-by-fours. "In case you need to, uh, defend yourself . . ."

Marnie remembered attacking Leah with a two-by-four. She said tersely, "No. I'm bringing Yertle."

Did the Elf grin for a second there? Marnie hoped not. This was not the slightest bit funny.

"All right," she said. "Why don't you go stand by the bottom of the stairs, in that alcove there? Take a two-by-four, and if anyone comes down who's not me, just—just—"

"Whack 'em," said the Elf. "Okay. Sure. Why not?"

Marnie eyed him suspiciously, but he looked serious enough. She helped him into position. It took less than a minute, but by the end his forehead had picked up a sweaty sheen again, and he definitely wasn't smiling. Marnie didn't look down at the makeshift bandage on his leg. She knew it was there. And she knew it was a lot more difficult to whack someone here in the real world than it was in cyberspace. She had already tried it.

"I'll get help," she whispered. "I promise. We're going to make it."

The Elf nodded. Marnie felt his eyes on her as she picked up the bucket. She held it carefully by the body, not the handle, and imagined hurling the contents in Leah's face. She looked at the stairs and took a deep breath. "Bye for now," she said to the Elf, and put her foot lightly on the first step.

"Marn," said the Elf suddenly.

Marnie wanted to go *now*. Just go, get whatever was to happen over with. It was all she could do to turn back toward the Elf. "What?"

He was leaning against the wall of the alcove at the foot of the stairs. He opened his mouth to say something and then appeared to change his mind. He frowned. After another moment he said, "I just wanted to point out—this is where we met. Right here, on these stairs. Historic place."

Marnie swallowed. Half-smiled. "Maybe we can install a plaque someday."

The Elf nodded. Marnie turned away again. "Good luck, Marn," said the Elf then, softly. It was a peculiar moment to realize that she didn't mind her name rhyming with barn, after all. He could call her anything he pleased. Capulet, Montague. What's in a name—

The realization hit her and she froze on the stairs. Unable to help herself, she whirled back, her lips parting to blurt out the sudden, urgent question.

His eyes . . . His eyes were so amazing. And he was looking at her as if . . . as if . . .

Marnie held his gaze. She swallowed again. She felt as if she were being flayed. At this moment, she could not remind him that she had never bothered to . . .

Romeo and Juliet had been wrong, of course, that balcony night. A name was more than a collection of letters; it was a symbol of the core of your identity. Skye had known that. Anyone who wanted to know *you* would want, would need, to know your true name. It mattered; oh, it mattered, and she, Marnie Skyedottir, she . . .

She had not asked the Elf's name.

She tore her eyes away.

She felt his on her back all her silent way up the stairs.

CHAPTER
29

With each footstep up the stairs, Marnie felt her pulse increase its speed. It pounded at her throat. She tried to think of a logical plan but was unable to come up with more than a single tenet: be ready to improvise.

Be ready to improvise.

The sentence raced hard through her blood. Her fingers tingled; her muscles tensed. All at once Marnie felt as if the Sorceress were looking out of one eye and she the other; and yet, somehow, they were perfectly coordinated in mind and body. She held Yertle firmly, and heard, shockingly, the Sorceress's low laughter.

Then her whisper: *We're ready.*

Marnie reached the top of the stairs and entered the living room, where, vividly, she could sense the living presence of Leah Slaight. Could feel her breathing. That presence pulled her, strong and sure, as a compass point is pulled north. There was no way around this confrontation. She didn't even think of trying to avoid it. She knew she could not.

Sometimes your fate is your fate, Skye had written.

Marnie moved through the sitting area, past its shabby sofa. Past the incongruously big, new television. Past a coffee table piled high with catalogs. Marnie had never felt so inexorably compelled to keep moving, moving. Moving toward the open archway between the living room and the kitchen. Moving toward Leah Slaight. Moving toward her fate—and the Elf's.

Marnie stopped.

"Hello," Leah said tightly. She was seated at the kitchen table, facing Marnie. Beyond her, Marnie could see the door of the house. On the other side of it lay hope, freedom, rescue. But between Marnie and the door sat Leah Slaight, with her elbows on the table and her gun in her right hand.

The gun was aimed, steadily, at Leah's own head.

Marnie heard herself utter a tiny sound.

But that's her *head, not ours!* screamed the Sorceress, suddenly divorced from Marnie. *Throw Yertle! So what if the gun goes off while she's aiming it at herself? Think of your own life, think of the Elf's.*

At the same time, Marnie heard Leah say, "Put that stinking bucket down, then sit. We need to talk."

Throw Yertle! Who cares if she's hurt? Don't wimp out on me . . . on the Elf . . .

Marnie took a deep breath. She knew that the Sorceress was right. Again. But what she was able to do instinctively in the heat of a fight was something

187

quite other than what she found she could do now, with Leah aiming the gun at her own head.

She watched Leah smile and knew that somehow the woman had understood her thoughts. Marnie was filled with hatred for Leah; she thought of the Elf in the basement, crippled, counting on her; and still she couldn't . . .

"Sit down," Leah said again. "I can talk more easily that way."

"I don't want to talk," Marnie heard herself say. "I want to go home. Will you just let us leave? Isn't that why you unlocked the door downstairs?"

Actually Marnie had no idea why Leah had unlocked the basement room and slipped back upstairs to wait. Unless—her stomach lurched—it was to make Marnie, and only Marnie, witness her suicide.

"I did it," said Leah patiently, "because I wanted you to come talk to me, alone. I knew you'd come. Now *sit down*. Or I'll—" Her fingers seemed to tighten on the gun.

Marnie spoke quickly, too quickly, and her voice went high. "Why should I care if you shoot yourself?" she said to Leah.

Why should you? whispered the Sorceress.

Leah looked back at Marnie steadily. "I know you don't believe I'm your sister," she said. "I've realized that. But I know that I am. And I know you better than you think—because I know Skye. You won't want my blood on your hands. Not this way." Unexpectedly, eerily, she grinned, and the muscle movement made the gun's mouth seem to shift closer to her temple.

Marnie did not make a conscious decision. But suddenly she found she had placed the bucket on the table and sat down across from Leah.

"I really hate you," she said evenly.

"That bucket stinks," said Leah, wrinkling her nose. Then, smoothly, she moved her gun arm and aimed the weapon directly at Marnie.

Marnie ceased to breathe. She was vaguely aware of the Sorceress snarling viciously in her inner ear. She knew herself for a weak fool. Elf, she thought. Max. And then: I'm sorry.

But then, bizarrely, Leah looked at her own hand, frowned as if she had momentarily lost her train of thought, smoothly shifted the gun back toward her own head, and actually shrugged as if in apology.

The silence stretched. And stretched. Marnie was very aware of Yertle. And of the Sorceress, her point proven, waiting impatiently for Marnie to act.

"You know what I want from you," Leah said.

Marnie did. And suddenly intolerant of the danger, she burst out: "Yes, but nothing I say can change who you are or aren't! I don't even understand why you'd *want* to be Skye's daughter. It's not an easy thing to be. Can't you see that—" She stopped. Leah Slaight was so full of need that she was incapable of seeing any such thing.

All those sessions on kidnappers, and not one had covered dealing with someone like Leah Slaight.

And what if Leah changed the direction of her gun again? It would only take a second, and Marnie was so close . . . And the Elf was downstairs, waiting . . . except that now Marnie had a horrible certainty he wouldn't stay there, not as the relative silence continued. She could almost see him limping grimly up the stairs.

Your fault if he lands in more danger, whispered the Sorceress viciously.

"Before," said Leah, "you *told* me you'd be my sister." She repeated aggressively: "You promised me, on Skye's soul."

Marnie tried to absorb this. She supposed there was a distinction between being Skye's daughter and Marnie's soul-sworn sister . . . maybe. Was that what Leah was getting at? Oh, Marnie's head hurt. Her throat was dry. Her heart was pounding as if it would burst from her chest in a bloody mess. She didn't know what to do.

Leah was looking at her as if Marnie held the keys to the universe. Marnie wondered how much time had passed. A few minutes? It felt like forever.

And this feeling of déjà vu. They had been here before; they had been exactly here before, she and Leah Slaight. No. She, and Leah, and Skye. And Skye had . . .

All at once the fear and discomfort seemed to drop away from Marnie. And within her a warmth bloomed small and then spread into calm, calm. She leaned forward instinctively and looked into Leah's mad, sad eyes.

She didn't think. She didn't need to think. She said, quietly, in a voice that was not quite her own: "Doesn't anyone love you, Leah Slaight?" And when Leah looked back at her, wearing the same expression that Marnie knew she herself had worn when the Elf had said . . . what he had said, Marnie opened her mouth and sang, huskily:

190

There is no place for her
No one who cares for her
What need is there for her
She's still a girl but it is over
Nothing ever was in order
Leah knows she can't discover
Why
Is there a rhyme, is there a reason?
If there's a God, where is She sleeping?
And why
Does anyone know why
Will someone please say why
Will someone just ask why
Will someone just ask why

The last words drifted from Marnie's lips. Leah's hand, she saw, was trembling now. Her cheeks were wet, and so, Marnie realized, were her own. She was vaguely aware of astonishment—she hadn't known she knew all the words to that song. She felt as if she were not quite in her body, as if she were outside. Watching. Listening. Feeling.

She looked into Leah's dark eyes. "Why, Leah? Why?"

Marnie didn't know what question she was asking. Which "why" she meant. There were so many. The situational whys—why had Leah fixated on Skye, on Marnie; why had Leah become who she was; what forces had taken her to this place, at this time?—but also the bigger questions. Skye-type questions. Why was there pain at all? Why was anyone alone, unloved? Why couldn't one person simply connect to another; why was it so complicated?

And why did desperate measures—measures of terror, like Leah's; or passive-aggressive methods like Marnie's—seem sometimes the only way to tell the world that you existed, that you mattered?

Was that what Leah had been trying to say, somehow?

But she's dangerous, whispered the Sorceress in despair. *Don't forget . . . she's dangerous . . . you're not like her! Don't be a fool. . . .*

I'm not a fool, Marnie thought, out of that deep sureness. Trust me, Sorceress.

Leah's gun hand was still shaking, but Marnie couldn't tell what she was thinking. Marnie took a breath, and then said, starkly: "Give me the gun. We both know you don't really want to hurt anyone. Not me; not yourself. We can work out the rest. I promise—I promise for real—that I will help. On Skye's soul, Leah. I *promise.*"

This time she meant it. She held her breath. She held out her hand.

And there was a moment. A moment when Leah's eyes flickered, and Marnie could tell, could feel, that she was thinking about it, was wondering if she could risk it. A moment in which Marnie knew, *knew,* that Leah wanted nothing more in this world than to put down her gun and believe that she could start again.

But then the moment passed.

Leah said, calmly, almost sorrowfully, "I'm sorry I shot that boy. He shouldn't have come. This was between you and me. And Her." Marnie could hear the capital letter. "She's the only one who can tell us the truth. We need to talk to Her. Both of us."

Marnie's hand was still outstretched. It began to shake. Within her, she felt her sympathy for Leah—the curious warmth toward the woman—retreat completely.

And she felt the Sorceress tense.

Okay, she told the Sorceress. Now. Now you are right.

Leah's gun arm began to swing outward. "If we can't be sisters alive, then—"

I will kill you, Marnie thought with a pure clarity that she had never before experienced. If I can, I will.

Now!

She grabbed Yertle with both hands and hurled the contents in Leah's direction, simultaneously shoving her chair back and throwing herself across the table toward Leah. Just as she did so, she was hit by the impact of a body, a big body, knocking her sideways off the table, landing familiarly on top of her. The Elf, the macho nitwit—

And then the gun exploded, just as the kitchen door burst open with a tremendous crash and Marnie heard someone's agonized shout: "Marnie!"

Max, she thought tiredly, dully. Max, with the cavalry.

A second too late.

CHAPTER 30

I t took Marnie three days of quasinormal routine at Halsett Academy to realize that the cancerous, constantly mutating knot of feelings and images involving Leah Slaight were not just going to disappear. The clues were small but definite. A constant low-level anxiety. A tightness in the small of her back. A nagging headache. The insane certainty that someone was watching her . . . hating her. She'd caught herself staring suspiciously at teachers, at other girls, even at Mrs. Fisher.

And then there was the image she saw whenever she closed her eyes. Leah's body. What was left of her head. Yet the visual memory was not the worst thing. The worst thing was the music that was attached to the memory. That played, softly, in her inner ear behind what she saw.

Skye's voice. Skye's song. Attached to Leah Slaight.

Other memories from those confused minutes—the first sight of Max; the reassuring presence of what looked like some kind of special operations team; the way Marnie hadn't, at first, been able to let go of the Elf; the seeping, astounding knowledge that neither of them had been hurt; even the utterly indescribable series of expressions that flitted across Max's face when he recognized the Elf—all of this faded, in the end, beside the fact of Leah Slaight.

Leah Slaight, dead by her own hand.

Sitting on the edge of her dorm bed, Marnie's stomach squeezed; turned over.

You survived, said the Sorceress sharply, and Marnie sighed. Yes. She looked at the door of her room, which she now left ajar at all times. She winced. Every day—at least once—she tried to shut that door but couldn't. Just couldn't.

The corridor outside was semidark now, at after ten at night. Absently she fingered her new necklace. It was rather gorgeous—a strong, twisted silver chain from which an amethyst geode hung suspended—and the fitting that held the geode also concealed an emergency signal button. "Oh, of course," Marnie had joked with Max. "I've seen something like this advertised for senior citizens who live alone." The weight of the geode felt reassuring against her skin, beneath her shirt. She imagined obtaining other James Bond devices. Homing beacons inserted beneath the skin. Winged cars. Strange poisons held in lockets—well, no, that would be more Paliopolis than Bond. She felt the corners of her lips turn up for a second before dropping back into a straight line. She glanced over at her computer. It sat on her desk as if it had never been gone. But she didn't move toward it.

One day at a time, the specialist counselor said. Max said. Mrs. Fisher said. The dean said. Even the Elf said.

Marnie thought about calling the Elf. Frank. Frank Delgado, although she kept having to remind herself of his name. She had called him, or he her, every one of the last few nights, since Marnie had been discharged from the hospital and returned, at her own insistence, to Halsett. The Elf—Frank— had gone home from the hospital today. Marnie had his phone number, but what if his mother answered? She had picked up the telephone in his hospital room this very afternoon. Marnie's shoulders tightened defensively, remembering. It was remarkable how much the Elf's mother had managed to say to Marnie, silently, in that single, little pause after Marnie identified herself.

He too had been . . . different today. Looking forward, for the first time, rather than back. "Listen, Marn," he'd said, with excitement ringing clearly in his voice. "College letters just came, and I got in everywhere I applied—even Harvard! I've still got to work out some money things, weigh up who's offering what in scholarships before deciding for sure, but . . ." Marnie wasn't surprised to hear about the college letters—their receipt and the attendant excitement and disappointment had been all over Halsett Academy that day too—but somehow, listening to his voice as he spoke about it deepened the sensation that he was rapidly moving away from her, returning to his regularly scheduled life. The life that included college plans, and buddy Dave, and, yes, that angry, frightened, possessive mother. By next September, he'd be at Harvard or wherever. There'd be girls there—lots of them. Smart girls, who got good grades. Shrewd girls, who'd see past the bald head. Pretty girls, wearing preppy clothes. Nice girls, whom his mother would like.

Marnie felt her lips twist into a vicious little smile, because even so, there was no way the Elf would ever forget Marnie Skyedottir. It had to be a rule of the universe that you never forgot the girl for whom you took your first bullet. In fact, Marnie could imagine it quite clearly: the Elf would be with some girl, in his dorm room at college, with the door closed, and the girl would locate the Elf's bullet wound and murmur, "Frank? What's this?"

No. Better to think of something else. Anything else. No, wait, not anything. Not Leah.

Not Skye.

The phone rang. Marnie grabbed it. "Hello?" She had to clear her throat. "Hello?" A second later, she blinked away her momentary, stupid disappointment. "Hi, Max," she said. "No, no. I wasn't asleep . . . Yeah, I did sleep some last night . . . Yeah, it helps to have someone to talk to. Definitely. Yeah, I think she's pretty nice, for a psychiatrist . . . Yeah . . ."

Max had offered to take her back to New York, to let her leave Halsett forever, but Marnie had said no. "I'm not running," she said to him, with—she realized—too much defiance in her voice. It hadn't been aimed at Max, though. Not this time. And he'd known it, she thought. He had just looked at her and, after a long minute, nodded, shoving his hands in his pockets.

He was still nearby, at the Halsett Inn, and Marnie knew security was not going to stop with the emergency necklace. That there was a body-guard in her immediate future. She wanted not to want one. She wanted to believe the necklace was enough. With her head, she did. Her gut, however, screamed a different story.

Maybe she would take up karate.

Max was trying really hard. It almost hurt Marnie to see how hard Max was trying. How guilt-ridden he felt. It turned out that he, and several security experts, had arrived in Halsett within twenty-four hours after Marnie disappeared. One of the so-called experts had even visited Leah Slaight's house right away, talked with Leah, and left again. Marnie figured it must have been while she herself was largely unconscious, ill, in the basement room.

"I am going to bankrupt that security firm," Max had said in that drawl of his. "I am going to sue them within an inch of their lives."

Marnie had found herself looking at him, realizing that beneath his anger he was blaming himself. She had wanted to soothe him but hadn't known how. Finally she'd replied feebly, "But since there was no ransom note . . . I can see how it made sense for everyone to start looking for a runaway—focus on train and bus stations, and the air-ports . . ."

But Max had compressed his lips. He had said, "No." And then, after a minute: "It's my fault. I should have known you better. Somebody—some adult—should have known you better. Not just that Delgado boy. If he hadn't parked his car nearby . . . if his mother hadn't filed a missing persons report and raised Cain . . ." He had stood up and turned away.

Marnie found that she couldn't, after all, raise the question about Leah, about Skye. Couldn't mention the one fleeting expression on Leah's face that had given her pause, made room for doubt. Not yet.

She clung to the phone now and listened to Max. Today he had been interviewing bodyguards. There was one candidate he wanted Marnie to meet. "Okay," she found herself saying. "Sure. I could meet him tomorrow afternoon, after classes." She wondered briefly where the bodyguard would live, but with Max in this mood, she wouldn't be surprised to see Tarasyn Pearce moved out of her room tomorrow and the bodyguard moved in. Or an entire dorm built just for Marnie and her guards. Marnie's mind suddenly conjured up the Palace of the Wicked Witch in *The Wizard of Oz*, complete with chanting. *Ooo—eeeee—oo! Yooo—ho! Ooo—eeeee—oo!* Yeah, that would be quite the campus sight. Here comes the wicked Sorceress with her flying monkeys. Luckily, Marnie already owned a lot of black clothing . . . she'd just need a hat . . . a broom—make it an electric broom, with a hypoallergenic dust filtering system.

"Uh, I'm sorry. What'd you say?" Marnie asked Max. "Oh, four o'clock. Fine. That's fine. Okay. Okay, bye." She hung up and found herself looking, again, at her open door. Would she really want a bodyguard out there? Would that make her feel safe? She sighed. Maybe it would, but was that how she wanted to live? Would it form a habit she could never break for the rest of her life?

The rest of her life. Now, there was another frightening thought. Marnie remembered the Elf and his college plans. He seemed so sure of what he wanted, while she had never looked further than inheriting Skye's money one day. As if her own worth could be measured only in dollars. As if Skye's inheritance were worth no more than that.

Oh, and there was the headache again. And . . . Skye, again.

"All her fault," Marnie muttered.

Oh, really, my pretty? said the Sorceress, cackling like the Wicked Witch of the West.

CHAPTER 31

"Okay to sit here?" The words were soft but also, yes, a little hostile. Or . . . something. Marnie felt her shoulders tense over her breakfast mug of hot chocolate and knew a quick moment of gladness for this morning's reflexive application of makeup and hair gel.

Jenna Lowry was standing a few feet away, across the table and two seats down. The rest of Marnie's table was empty, as was most of the dining hall. With nearly an hour before the first class of the day, few students had yet shown up for breakfast.

"Go ahead," Marnie replied warily.

Jenna sat down with her tray, pulled the cap off a purple highlighter, and, after taking a bite of marmalade toast, buried herself in a ragged book. Marnie noted, sourly, that this wasn't a book whose cover Jenna felt she needed to conceal. *Jane Eyre.* Still romance, though, even if certified Literature.

Marnie wondered if Jenna had made up with hockey boy.

Head still down, Jenna said abruptly, "This must be such a hard time for you. Everyone was so shocked. It seems incredible, Ms. Slaight being so crazy and locking you up. I even heard she thought she was your sister. And then killing herself, and you being there. I mean, I know it's true and all, but I still almost don't believe it. Not here at Halsett. You know what I mean? Does it seem like a dream to you? Or . . . a nightmare, I guess."

"Yeah," Marnie managed. "It's like a bad movie."

She could almost hear the echo of the dean's words at the assembly. *I deeply regret the part our school has played in this tragedy. I can promise all of you, as I have promised your parents, that we shall closely review our hiring and safety policies, although certainly when I search my conscience I can find no way in which we could have predicted or prevented the peculiar events of this past week.*

Marnie shook her head to banish the words. She had the feeling the dean would be thrilled to get rid of her. That was another thing Marnie wasn't ready to think about: what she'd do if she didn't stay here. The subject panicked her. Ironic, given how much she'd once wanted to leave.

"Awful for you," said Jenna. She looked up finally, but only for a second. "I'm just so sorry. I, um—we were all worried about you. While you were gone."

Marnie felt all her hackles rise. Jenna *had* to say that. Everybody had to say it. How was Marnie supposed to reply? "I, uh, appreciate it," she said.

Jenna dove back into her book—with relief, Marnie noted.

A page crackled as Jenna attacked her book with the highlighter. Marnie could actually hear the swoosh of the pen's thick nub moving across the page as Jenna highlighted line after line. She wondered what scene Jenna found so worthy of note. She wondered, was Jenna planning to apply to Harvard too? Lots of Halsett girls did. If Jenna went there, would she meet the Elf? Would she have the insight, given her hockey boy, to even appreciate someone like the Elf?

Don't start that, warned the Sorceress.

Marnie sighed. She pulled her eyes from Jenna and returned them to the depths of her own mug. She spooned up a little hot chocolate, swallowed it, and turned her thoughts inward again, away from Jenna and the Elf.

The counselor had said, "Marnie, it may take a long time, months, possibly even years of careful examination and analysis and anger and mourning before you feel any sense of real closure. But it is over. Leah Slaight is dead. She killed herself, and she can't harm you anymore. Indeed, she harmed mostly herself. One day, dear, you will believe it with your heart as well as your head."

Dear. Once, Marnie would have verbally scalded this stranger for calling her dear. Once, she would have had a smug, lengthy, cross-indexed internal list of all the things this counselor had got wrong, didn't understand, could *never* understand.

What else was it that the counselor had said? That, in the meantime, life had to be lived.

But how? What did people *mean* when they said that? And . . . what did she, Marnie Skyedottir, want? She'd always been so focused on what she didn't want. She had another flashing image of the Palace Guards, and shuddered. She felt she should do something, *something*, but she didn't know what . . .

"What did you say?" asked Jenna.

Marnie blinked. She met Jenna's stare. "What?"

"You said something."

"No, I didn't."

Their eyes dueled. Eventually Jenna hunched a shoulder and returned to her toast and her book. Bearing down hard, she highlighted another sentence or five.

Marnie had lost her train of thought, anyway. She asked loudly, "What did you just highlight?"

Jenna looked up. "What?"

"What did you just highlight?"

Jenna's mouth twisted. "What do you care?"

"I'm just curious," Marnie said. To her amazement, she found she was. The honesty sounded in her voice. Jenna looked at her, uncertain.

"Please," said Marnie. The word surprised her—and Jenna, she thought.

After a couple of seconds, Jenna shrugged. "Fine." She took in a deep breath and looked down at her book, eyelids flickering as she scanned the passage. Her shoulders moved uneasily, and for an instant Marnie thought she wasn't going to read it after all. But then all at once Jenna lifted her chin and began, using a low voice that grew in depth and clarity as she went on, as if she could not help reciting well.

"This is Jane talking, okay? 'You are a married man—or as good as a married man, and wed to one inferior to you—to one with whom you have no sympathy—whom I do not believe you truly love; for I have seen and heard you sneer at her. I would scorn such a union: therefore I am better than you.'"

Jenna flung out the last sentence intensely, meaningfully, as if hurling it at a lover in a quarrel, and Marnie found herself suddenly sure that hockey boy was a thing of the past.

Jenna was now looking down thoughtfully, pushing at the toast on her plate. There was self-conscious color in her cheeks.

"Jaysus," Marnie drawled. She was sorry even before Jenna's head snapped up.

"You never change, do you?" Jenna spat. "Even a near-death experience doesn't change you. Well, I'm tired of it." She jumped to her feet, grabbed her book and her tray, and left.

Well, said the Sorceress after a minute. *What was that all about?*

I have no idea why she—

Not her. You. You asked her to open up and then you slapped her.

Marnie moved her shoulders uncomfortably. She imagined that everyone else in the dining hall was looking at her now. Well, fine. Let them look. They always had.

Her hot chocolate had gone cold. She clenched

her fingers around it anyway. Jenna Lowry was a snobby, mean jerk and always had been. Right? Nothing had changed. Nothing had changed at Halsett, so why should Marnie change? Why?

With a new lurch of the stomach, she remembered that she had dreamed again last night. Now it all came back in a rush, playing in her mind's eye as if it had been captured on film.

The Rubble-eater, coming closer. Llewellyne's sword, posed. The trembling, and the knot of fear in her throat. And then—

The beast suddenly accelerating out of its normal lumbering run and swerving to leap, with the full force of its heavy body, headfirst toward the sharp end of the sword.

The sickening ease with which the sword entered the Rubble-eater's eye and thrust deep into its brain.

The scene replayed once, twice, as if in a loop, and Marnie shuddered.

The bell rang for first period. Marnie looked up. The dining hall was empty again, except for her.

CHAPTER 32

Right after classes, as soon as she'd sat down in the conference room near the dean's office with Max and the bodyguard candidate, all at once Marnie did know one thing she could do, and she fell upon the idea with relief. Since the autopsy was over, there was no time to be lost, so she immediately blurted it out. "Max—about Leah Slaight. I want us to give her a funeral. A real one, with a minister and everything. Can we do that?" She thought of the memorial service for Skye. Of how numb she'd been then. And how small; how young; how lacking in the ability to ask for anything . . .

The potential bodyguard, at whom Marnie had merely nodded before speaking, pulled back slightly from the table and pasted an I-listen-but-do-not-hear look on his face. In a subsidiary compartment of her mind Marnie wondered if he might work out after all. Perhaps for a short time. *Ooo—eeeee—oo!* A very short time, she hoped.

Max was clearly taken aback. After a moment, he said, "But she—it's not our body to claim."

"You told me her adoptive family refused to claim her."

"You needn't worry about that. The state will take care of—"

"That's not good enough." On top of the table, Marnie's hands intertwined and tightened.

There was a pause. Max's gaze flicked to Marnie's hands and then back to her face. Finally he spoke, but carefully, as if he were walking on glass. "Marnie. It seems to me that possibly you're feeling responsible for this woman, and I want you to know there's no need for that."

Marnie bit her lip and glanced down, away from Max's intent focus. He said to the bodyguard, "Would you excuse us for a few minutes?" And when the man had left, Max said, "Marnie, I wasn't as clear as I could have been on a certain point earlier. At the time I thought it wasn't necessary. That you wouldn't for a second believe . . . Hmm. Anyway. Now I think that we—I—need to be clear. This woman, um . . ." He paused, and all at once Marnie's fists clenched.

"Her name," Marnie said distinctly, "is Leah. *Was* Leah. Leah Slaight."

For a second Max's jaw tightened. But he continued smoothly enough: "Believe me, Marnie, I know her name. What I want to say is that she—Ms. Slaight—was mistaken in her allegations that she was Skye's daughter, your sister. Mistaken. That is to say, wrong." Max's voice sharpened. "I will admit that her mistake was tragic. I'm not without sympathy for any deranged individual. But I have not forgotten that she endangered you—not to mention, um, young Mr. Delgado.

"And I want to make sure that, out of some misplaced sympathy, you don't start imagining things that aren't true. You are Skye's only daughter. Only child. You must believe that, Marnie."

There was silence.

"I need to know that you're clear on this, Marnie," said Max. "On all of it. Are you? Marnie, do you understand what I'm saying?"

"I hear you," Marnie said softly, and for a moment stopped right there, suddenly feeling she had stumbled to the edge of a steep, jagged cliff. No matter; she would ignore her fear. She took in a breath and then leaped. "I just don't see why I should believe you."

Max's face went utterly blank.

"I don't see how you can possibly know for sure." Marnie swallowed. She felt a little as if she were hammering nails into Max's forehead. "I think . . . I think you're just assuming . . . or . . . or hoping . . . like I did, when she— when Leah—first told me. Because it would be messy. Because you think there's no point, maybe. Because you don't want to think Skye would have kept a secret like that. But the thing is, I don't know." She didn't add her other thought. That Max *might* know. That he might be lying to her, even now. For her own good, of course. He would believe it was for her own good.

209

Max was silent for so long that Marnie was sure she'd hit the truth. One way or another. She took a deep breath. She would ask for the genetic tests, she decided. She needed to know.

By the time Max spoke, his face had gone pasty. His voice, however, was rock steady. "I knew your mother as an adult, Marnie. Adult to adult. That's different from the way you knew her. Your perceptions are based on a child's recollections. You have to admit that. You can trust my judgment."

Oh, please. "And why is that, pray tell?" Marnie flashed. "Are you claiming you never get someone wrong? Never make mistakes? Adults are perfect, and *you're* especially perfect—is that what you're saying?"

Unexpectedly, Max flinched, as if she'd punched him in the stomach. Then he recovered. "No, I'm not . . . that is . . . the point is—Marnie, I'm not making a mistake here."

"No?" said Marnie. Inside, her stomach had begun to churn.

"No," said Max, and nothing else, even though—suddenly—the room was heavy with unspoken things. Marnie could feel them. And, for the first time, her need to know was stronger than her need not to.

"Fine. Believe what you want," she said. "But you can't make me believe anything. Not now. Not ever. Not without facts."

Abruptly she stood, pushing her chair back from the conference table. The chair skidded several feet from the force of her shove, nearly colliding with the wall.

"Marnie."

Something new in Max's voice. She stilled, and then, slowly, reluctantly, turned back.

"Please, can't you trust me on this, Marnie? Please, can't you? Won't you?"

Please. Twice. And that tone. She had never heard Max sound quite this anguished before. But it didn't matter. It couldn't be allowed to matter.

"No," Marnie said quietly. She remembered something the Elf had said to her. She said it to Max. "I have a right to know."

Max was silent. Looking at her. Looking at her. She looked back.

"What if we did do a genetic test?" Max said finally. "When it comes back negative, will you be satisfied? Will you believe in Skye again?"

Now, that was an odd question. Marnie found herself saying carefully, "I guess I would then believe that Leah Slaight wasn't my sister."

Max was silent again.

"Max?" Marnie said.

He pushed his own chair back, then, and turned it so that he faced her. "Marnie."

Marnie stared at him. There was something new, something frightening, in his voice. Her stomach pulsed and for a moment she thought she would need to run for the bathroom. But she couldn't seem to move, and the impulse passed.

"I *do* know for sure, Marnie," Max said. "I know exactly what Skye was doing, and where she was, during the time we're talking about. She did not have a baby then. It's not possible, Marnie. Do you hear me? It's completely impossible."

Max swallowed. But he looked directly into Marnie's eyes and his voice, again, was strong. "I'm going to tell you everything, Marnie. It was never meant to be a secret forever. Just until you were twenty-one."

In a strange, new calm, Marnie waited. She had a feeling that she'd been waiting . . . maybe forever.

"Skye was in a juvenile detention center for nearly three years, from fifteen until she turned eighteen."

Marnie's calm wavered. She opened her mouth but nothing came out. Her stomach churned. "She . . . she what? *What?*"

"She was in a medium-security girls' lockup," Max repeated. His mouth was a grim line. "In Mississippi. Her time there is completely accounted for, and is a matter of public record. Some girls do have babies in prison, but Skye did not."

Marnie said nothing. She kept hearing Max's words repeating in her mind. Kept hearing them, yes, but they seemed like gibberish. They didn't make any sense at all.

"Sit down," said Max after another moment. "And we'll deal with the rest of it. I'll explain everything. Marnie, I—"

Marnie put out one hand and waved it. Max stopped talking. She didn't know what she had expected—but not this. Surely not this. Everything she thought she'd known had shifted, again. She struggled for something to grab on to. Some fact. Some certainty. She found nothing.

Max got up, took Marnie's arm, and guided her

into his abandoned chair. He squatted awkwardly and looked her in the eye. He took her hand.

Marnie had no concept of how much time passed then. Finally, however, she managed to ask the obvious question, the one that—she knew—Max was waiting for. She hardly recognized her own voice.

"What was Skye in prison for?"

Now that Max had made up his mind to talk, he didn't waver. And he looked directly into Marnie's eyes.

"For murder, Marnie. Premeditated murder. First-degree murder."

CHAPTER 33

"Skye's name," Max said evenly, "was once Lea Hawkes." And when Marnie's eyes widened, he added, "It's spelled L, E, A."

Marnie thought of the song Skye had written, the one Leah Slaight had so identified with. Leah with an H. The more common spelling.

Max pulled up another chair. Once he'd settled in, he moved as if to take Marnie's hand again, but she pulled it back. Max cleared his throat. "Shall I go on?"

"Yes." Marnie was pleased with her voice. It was clear and calm. In her head she could feel the Sorceress's soothing presence. It made her feel as if she weren't alone, as if a wise friend were with her, listening also.

Lea Hawkes, of Full Moon, Mississippi, had been the illegitimate daughter of a local girl and an unknown father. When Lea was seven, her young mother ran away from Full Moon without her child, and Lea was sent to live in a foster home. By her teenage years, she was still in the same foster home but was not considered to have good prospects.

Marnie interrupted. "Let me guess. She was flunking out of school."

"Well," Max dithered, "it wasn't that she was stupid—"

"I know," said Marnie softly.

Did the corner of Max's mouth turn up ruefully for a second? Marnie couldn't be sure. If so, it immediately turned down again, and then Max looked away. There was a rather long pause before he resumed. "It wasn't just that she was skipping school all the time," he said. "It was what she was doing instead of studying. Not that anyone knew except me." He paused again, still not looking at Marnie. Then he added: "She was learning to shoot."

For a minute Marnie almost felt her eyes bug out of her head. Learning to shoot? *Skye?*

Max was staring into the distance. "She was using my rifle. I was ten. I told my father I'd lost it and I gave it to her. He whipped me for it but it was worth it.

"You see, I hated hunting. Always did. But my father . . . well, in any event." He cleared his throat. "And Lea Hawkes was my friend. She was nice to me, and in those days, not many people were. So when she asked me . . ." His voice drifted off and then strengthened. "I helped her at first, taught her everything I'd been taught, but she didn't need much help. And after two years of practice she was the best marksman in the county. Lea Hawkeye, I called her. It gave me a kind of thrill to think that she could outshoot my father if she wanted. I thought we were working toward a time when she'd just show them all. I was pretty confused, actually; I don't know why I thought that would prove anything to my father. About me, I mean. But it didn't matter anyway. That wasn't what Lea had in mind."

Max was watching his hands, but his voice was even now. "I told you Lea was my friend. But what I came to understand—later—is that I wasn't hers. Not then anyway, though later on . . . well, that's another story. But *then*, you see, she was playing for stakes I couldn't imagine. Or . . . not playing at all, I suppose. It was never a game."

Into the difficult pause, Marnie finally said carefully, "I—I see." Premeditated murder, Max had said. "She wanted to learn to shoot so she could kill someone specific. . . ." Marnie's voice trailed off.

"Her foster father," Max said quietly. "Since she was thirteen, her foster father had been raping her." He added, "I didn't know, of course." And then, with a touch of self-loathing: "Not that I was capable of doing anything if I had known."

There was silence, then, for some minutes. Oddly, Marnie found herself wondering how many times over the years Max had imagined himself telling this story to Marnie. How many times he had told it to himself . . .

"Marnie?" said Max. "It's difficult. I know it's difficult."

She could feel his eyes, but she couldn't look back just yet.

Please, she asked the Sorceress. Just—take over for a while, okay?

The Sorceress looked up calmly and met Max's eyes. "I'm okay, Max," she said. "You're right, it is a shock . . . but I think I always knew something bad must have happened to her."

Max looked dubious.

"Really," the Sorceress said. "It's better to know."

Max nodded, though his eyes said he didn't quite believe her. "You want me to tell you the rest now, or later?"

"Now," said the Sorceress, while Marnie stayed safe and quiet.

"She killed her foster father, as you guessed," Max said. "It might seem unfair that she went to prison for it. . . . She was only fifteen." He paused, and the Sorceress nodded. "But what you have to understand is that legally, it couldn't be considered self-defense. Self-defense is in response to a current threat to life. More importantly, it was first-degree murder because she planned it in advance. She spent two years figuring out how to do it, working every angle, setting things up, making sure it would look like a hunting accident. And it did. A stray bullet, hitting a habitually careless hunter who'd gone out, a little drunk, without his orange vest. She didn't use my rifle, by the way. She was too smart for that."

Marnie felt her eyes widen. Her composure began to fall away in bits. Plans. She was a planner, too, a strategist. A gamer.

217

Not now, whispered the Sorceress, correctly.

Marnie took a deep breath and refocused. I'll take over now, she told the Sorceress.

You're sure?

Yes.

Max had gone on. "Someday you can read her confession, Marnie. If you want to. It's in the public record in the Full Moon courthouse. She—it was really a rather brilliant plan. Went off without a hitch, too. Nobody suspected a thing."

Marnie said, "But how did she get caught, if nobody suspected?"

"She didn't get caught," Max said.

Marnie blinked. "I'm sorry?"

"She confessed. Four weeks after the murder, she walked into the local police station and told them everything. At first she had some trouble getting them to believe her, but she had proof—she had kept the murder weapon, a shotgun that she'd stolen from her foster father two years before. She pleaded guilty, so there was no trial; and they sent her straight to the juvenile lockup. She was released at eighteen—that was back when there was automatic lenience for juvenile offenders. On top of which, the court system—not to mention the town of Full Moon—had a lot of sympathy for her. We all believed her about the abuse. And I think we were all ashamed . . . that no one knew. That no one did anything . . . because afterward, it was so obvious . . . I know that I . . ."

Max stopped. He seemed to expect Marnie to say something.

Smoothly the Sorceress took over again. "Why did she confess? You said she'd have gotten away with it."

Max seemed relieved to have a question to address. "What she said to the police was that, in those weeks after committing murder, she did a lot of thinking. She said that that was when she found she did believe in God, after all. That she needed to clear her conscience and face her punishment." He hesitated, then looked directly into Marnie's eyes again. "What she said to me, also, later, was that this was when she began to change inside, from Lea Hawkes into Skye."

Yes, Marnie thought. It was what Skye would have done. Confess. Skye, not—not little Lea Hawkes.

She could feel the Sorceress's agreement.

"Another thing to know," Max said, "the people of Full Moon were good to Skye. Not just by being sympathetic when she confessed, but after she got out, after she changed her name. When Skye became a gospel singer, and then a writer, and became so well known . . . well, there were a few occasions when people—newspeople—tried to find out her background. And the Full Moon folks, they knew perfectly well that Skye was Lea Hawkes, but nobody ever told.

"Skye has friends there, Marnie. Well . . . what I'm trying to say . . . it's not the same as having a family, of course, but you have people in Full Moon, Marnie. People who feel connected to Skye and to you. I have two sisters. . . . It's a small town, maybe a little bit of an odd town. But someday you might want to go there. Meet people."

The Sorceress whispered a sudden, urgent question to Marnie. Marnie was feeling too numb to do more than repeat it. "My father?"

Max shook his head. "I don't know, Marnie. That secret she kept."

Oh, said the Sorceress.

"Oh," echoed Marnie.

Max said hesitantly, "You do realize—whoever your father was, it wouldn't have been a big romantic thing. Your mother knew a lot about love, in a way, but she didn't seem ever to want to risk an intimate relationship. I think—well . . . well . . . well, I don't know. But—you know?"

"Yeah," Marnie said softly. Oddly, she was feeling stronger suddenly, as if she'd been transported back to familiar ground. She thought of her old sperm bank theory. "I do know, Max. Don't worry."

A pause. And then: "I do worry," said Max bluntly. "Every minute. Every day."

Marnie looked at him then. For a split second she had a sensation of what a weight, what a very great weight Max had been shouldering all this time. She raised her chin. "Thanks, Max," she said, and thought he probably understood.

She wanted, terribly, to be alone. Well, alone with the Sorceress. "Is that all of it?"

Max nodded.

Marnie wet her lips. "I still want a funeral," she said steadily. "For Leah Slaight."

After only a second, Max said, "Okay. We can do that."

"Thanks," said Marnie. And then, after another long minute, she added: "Max?"

"Yes?"

But found, after all, that she didn't have words. So she said again, feebly, "Thanks."

Max stared bleakly at her, and tried to smile.

CHAPTER 34

Marnie walked back toward her dorm on automatic pilot. *Oh my God,* the Sorceress kept whispering, and Marnie's churning stomach spoke her agreement. She tried to breathe deeply, to keep from stumbling, while thoughts assaulted her. Now that Max wasn't present, she couldn't keep from imagining it, all of it. . . .

Lea, not Skye. Lea. Lea Hawkes, only thirteen. Younger than Marnie was now, and small, and alone. And then that man, whoever he was . . . In her mind, Marnie could see the back of his head, his hunting jacket, his big hands—but not his face. She swallowed. She didn't want to imagine his face, and she wouldn't. She *wouldn't.*

Still, she had to stop for a moment, in the empty hall just inside her dorm, and put out a hand to lean against the wall.

She couldn't see the man's face, but she could see

Lea Hawkes's, and clearly. Expression concealed by shaggy dark hair, behind which watched Skye's eyes. No, not Skye's eyes. Not so sad, not so wise, not so loving as Skye's. Lea's eyes were bewildered. Scared. Helpless, and aware, very aware, of her helplessness.

Then, in Marnie's vision, those childish eyes changed. They were wary now. Watchful, missing nothing. Planning eyes now. Planning . . .

In a quick flash of her imagination, Marnie saw Lea's thin teenage arm snake out and snatch her foster father's rifle to hide away.

Marnie leaned more fully against the wall. Oh, little Lea, she thought. Little Lea . . .

She was brave, said the Sorceress insistently. *Brave and smart. You see that, don't you? Not a victim! You see that? Marnie, you see that?*

Yes, Marnie saw. But she saw more, too. She put her forehead against the cool painted concrete of the wall. Little Lea Hawkes, smart, brave Lea Hawkes, who had found the sheer guts and nerve within herself to transform from prey to predator.

A necessary transformation? Maybe. Yes. Oh, yes. But what became of a predator once she existed? How did she live?

What she said to me was that this was when she began to change inside, from Lea Hawkes into Skye.

Marnie closed her eyes tightly. I don't understand, she thought desperately. I don't understand, but I need to understand.

She felt her breath come out of her in a sob. It was beyond her. It was *beyond* understanding. She didn't know what to think, what to feel, what to do. She wished suddenly, fiercely, that she were exhausted enough to drop into a deep dreamless sleep, right here, right now . . . because in another minute she would scream and scream, and maybe she would never, never stop. . . .

At that moment, a hand fell uncertainly on Marnie's shoulder. "What's wrong? You weren't at dinner . . ." The voice was sharp, reluctant. Familiar.

And, somehow, hearing Jenna Lowry's voice brought Marnie back into reality. Breathing carefully, she fumbled for a grip on herself, and got it. Then, when she was ready, she swiped her cheeks with the back of her hand and straightened, defiantly, to face Jenna.

Jenna, ponytailed, was wearing sweats and running shoes. She took in Marnie's face and her eyes widened. She opened her mouth.

Marnie found words first—casual words, designed to tell Jenna she was pretending everything was normal, and to suggest that Jenna ought to do the same. "Hi, Jenna. Going running?" Her voice shook on the greeting, strengthened on the question.

Reflexively Jenna nodded. She hesitated, shrugged, and half-turned away. Then she snapped back around to face Marnie. "You—uh—should I go get—"

Marnie was staring at Jenna's worn running shoes. She meant only to cut her off, firmly and definitely. But the words she actually said shocked herself, instead. "Can I come with you?"

The moment she'd said it, she knew that she—Marnie Skyedottir, superslug—wanted nothing more passionately right now than lengthy, hard physical exercise.

Jenna's mouth had dropped open.

Marnie added, "Please? It'll only take me a couple minutes to change."

She knew Jenna didn't want her. She knew it.

"Okay," said Jenna. "I'll wait outside."

"I'm doing a three-mile loop this evening," Jenna said as they stretched. "But you shouldn't do that much; you're not used to it. A mile is plenty. There's a turnoff at around half a mile where you can double back. And another at one and a quarter."

Marnie nodded, but she knew she wouldn't use the turnoffs. Adrenaline pulsed through her veins. She fell into step beside Jenna and they began to jog. When Jenna picked up speed, her longer legs stretching out, Marnie matched her stride.

They ran in silence, leaving the campus behind and heading away from town on a secondary dirt road. Their feet pounded steadily. Overhead, trees were beginning to leaf, and the air was warm as the sun moved steadily toward the horizon. Within a few minutes Marnie slowed long enough to pull off her sweatshirt and tie it around her waist. Then she caught up again to the more lightly clad Jenna.

"The first turnoff's coming up," Jenna said after several minutes. "You want to loop back?"

"No," Marnie panted. She felt, rather than saw, Jenna's shrug. Distantly, as if it were happening to someone other than herself, Marnie was aware that her legs were already sore, her lungs laboring in the early-evening air. But it didn't matter. She could go on. She wanted to go on. Without noticing, she sped up a little, and Jenna kept pace.

They reached the second turnoff. "You still okay?" asked Jenna.

Marnie thought she would have an asthma attack. Her left calf was screaming; the right one merely moaned. "Yes." She barely got the word out, but she picked up the pace again anyway.

They ran on. Marnie could hear her breath wheezing in and out of her lungs. Her heart was pounding twice as fast as her feet. Jenna kept stealing looks at her but she ignored them. Kept on, kept on. There was a horrible pain in her left shin but she ignored it. She kept perfectly in pace with Jenna. Mind over matter. Remarkable. Everything had disappeared from her mind and body but the pain, and it was wonderful. Wonderful. She had no idea how much time had passed, how far they'd come. . . .

"Marnie, this is ridiculous!"

With difficulty, Marnie pulled herself out of her semitrance. "Can't. Talk."

"Well, you might hurt yourself. Let's walk awhile, okay?"

Marnie kept running. So did Jenna. Marnie wondered vaguely why she'd never been interested in this kind of thing before. Finally she'd found a way to make her mind just shut up. It was thoroughly occupied with alarm about her legs and lungs . . . with pain . . . lovely pain, numbing pain. Gasping, she increased her speed again.

Jenna grabbed her arm and skidded them both to a halt. "Marnie, stop it! I won't be a party to this."

Marnie wrenched free and ran on. She heard Jenna shouting after her but ignored it. After another minute, Jenna raced up beside her.

"Stop it! You utter bitch, just stop already! . . . Would you stop . . . you *have* to stop!" This time Jenna grabbed Marnie with both hands, and when Marnie tried to pull free again, Jenna threw herself on top of her. They tumbled to the ground. "Stop it!" Jenna said again, desperately. She rolled so that she was on top of Marnie's legs. "What's wrong with you? Stop it, stop it, stop it!"

Marnie's cheek lay in the dirt of the road. Her legs cramped violently. She suddenly stopped struggling and lay still. Her heart was beating wildly. She could hear it, feel it, almost taste it. For a moment she thought that only the fact that she was sprawled flat on her front would keep her heart from exploding out of her chest.

"I hate you." Jenna was crying now. Marnie could hear it. She closed her eyes and concentrated on her breathing. After a while she felt Jenna roll off her. As soon as she did, Marnie curled into a ball, trembling.

"Oh, God," Jenna whispered. "Marnie! Marnie, you have to get hold of yourself, we're miles from school. Marnie . . ."

Marnie thought of the Rubble-Eater, pounding its head against a wall. Leah Slaight, she had thought. But now . . .

"Marnie . . ."

Jenna sounded frantic. She was leaning over Marnie now. Shaking her. Saying all kinds of things that didn't penetrate, about school and trouble-making bitches and no excuses, intermixed with pleading diatribes about people who worried even though Marnie didn't deserve it, some babble about boyfriends and sonnets, and, of course, one frantic cry of that perennial favorite phrase of faculty and staff alike, who-the-hell-did-Marnie-think-she-was. And then Jenna pulled back her right hand and slapped Marnie hard, right across the face.

And then again. "Get a grip on yourself!" she yelled.

Marnie stared into Jenna's alarmed eyes. She sat up with difficulty and then touched her cheek. It stung. Her whole body . . . She felt something moist on her hand. Blood? She pulled down her hand and looked at her palm. No . . . there was more moisture on her cheeks; she could feel it. More and more. She blinked hard, but it didn't help. She stared at Jenna. She felt her shoulders begin to shake. Jenna was staring back, horrified, reaching out. "Marnie—"

Marnie buried her face in both her hands. Her shoulders shook even more. She heard a distant, low gasp and knew it had come from her own mouth. And then another, another. She couldn't stop shaking, she couldn't, couldn't, couldn't—

And then Marnie could feel Jenna's arms. Tight, warm, soothing, desperate. "I don't want to cry!" Marnie wailed.

"Tell someone who cares," said Jenna grimly. But

she held on. Marnie could feel Jenna's chin on her head. And then Jenna said something else, low. And then kept saying it over and over and over, with a catch in her own voice.

"I know. I know."

CHAPTER 35

Marnie felt shame and humiliation steal over her as soon as she stopped crying. She shook herself away from Jenna. Her legs ached so much that she wondered, remotely, if she'd even be able to get up. Her face felt swollen and blotchy. Her ears rang so that, when Jenna spoke, at first she thought she hadn't heard properly. Then she knew she had.

"We've got to stop meeting like this."

Marnie cautiously turned back toward Jenna. "Ha ha," she said huskily.

Just for a second, Jenna's face brightened with relief. Her eyes scanned Marnie's for clarity and found it. "You all right now?"

Marnie found she couldn't lie. She shrugged. "Well. Probably not."

Remarkably, Jenna flushed. "Sorry. Stupid question."

"No," Marnie found herself saying. "It's . . ."

She paused, thinking how inadequate the English language truly was. "It's okay. I mean, well . . ."

"Yeah, I know," said Jenna.

Silence. Marnie concentrated on massaging her calves. Jenna was keeping her distance now, which was good, but Marnie could feel her watching. Even feel her thinking. And when Jenna finally spoke, it was as if the words burst from her. "I know there's a lot going on with you—I mean, my God, being kidnapped and nearly killed and all—but I can't help wondering . . . just now . . . I mean, I know it's not my business, but I—was it your boyfriend? Something he . . . I'm sorry." She averted her face. "Not my business."

Somewhere in the middle of all this, Marnie had looked up sharply. Her boyfriend? Did Jenna mean the Elf? Er, Frank? But how would Jenna know— why would she assume . . . And then Marnie remembered Jenna crying that night . . . like Marnie now . . .

I know, Jenna had said. She didn't, but . . . but she *thought* she did.

Suddenly Marnie had to know. "Jenna, what *exactly* happened with hockey boy?"

Jenna looked bewildered. "Hockey boy?"

"Your boyfriend or whoever. You spent that weekend with him, right?" Marnie's voice was still husky, but somehow also peremptory. "Then you came back crying. And now you ask me about— anyway. What happened with hockey boy?"

Jenna's mouth had fallen open. Her hands reached to clutch her own arms. "I don't see why it's your business."

Marnie's voice went quieter. "I know it's not. I'm just asking. I want—that is, I—I could listen. If you want." And from somewhere, she knew to add: "And not tell anyone, ever, if that's what you want."

Jenna's chin was up. "Did you—are you . . . ?" She paused, searching for words, but Marnie didn't need them. Maybe this was what was meant by mind reading. When you were utterly focused on someone else, watching the tiny movements of their fingers, their eyebrows, the way they turned their head, and you knew even a little bit about them, you could tell what they were thinking . . . almost. . . .

"No," Marnie replied. And then, as if the words were pulled from her, she added: "I'm—for me . . . it's something to do with my mother. Today, I mean." She gestured aimlessly at her blotchy face. And then she blinked, astonished at how easily the words had emerged. How simple they were. But how inadequate . . . how almost silly . . . She hadn't said a thing, hadn't even begun to confide, not really . . . And yet . . .

"Oh," said Jenna. She had been watching Marnie as closely as, a moment ago, Marnie had been watching her. "I see." Jenna's voice was gentle. "You loved her? You miss her? Especially now, after—after last week?"

Marnie's mouth opened with something almost like shock. She stared at Jenna. It wasn't so simple. Was it? She felt her eyes begin to fill again. Her throat had completely closed, all at once, and yet it was important—vitally important—to answer

Jenna. To share, even this tiny little bit. But she couldn't speak.

She nodded instead. *Yes.*

Oh, yes.

She looked up after a moment to find Jenna watching her. For what was only a few seconds, and yet seemed like much longer, they looked at each other. Marnie found that her throat had loosened.

And then Jenna said, calmly, still looking straight at Marnie, "Well. Okay. About hockey boy. It's not what I think you're thinking. It's—I didn't even like him, you see. That was what was wrong." She paused. "I wanted a boyfriend. And he seemed to like me. Enough, anyway. And then . . ." She shrugged and looked away for an instant. "Stupid thing to get so upset about, huh? Nothing like what you've gone through . . . Anyway, there I was with him, and I suddenly realized. And when I told him, he got angry—which he should have, of course. *Stupid.* I was focused on all the wrong things."

"No," Marnie found herself saying. "Not stupid, Jenna." She knew what Skye would have said. "Human." But Jenna shook her head. "Okay, then," Marnie said. "At least no stupider than anyone else. Than, say, me."

Jenna's lips twisted. She seemed to be hesitating over something else she wanted to say. She wasn't looking at Marnie anymore. Finally she said it, almost in a whisper. "I felt so filthy. I can't describe it. I still feel it . . . all along I was condescending to him, and then, when I realized what I was doing . . . for no good reason, just because . . . I was the one who decided to go to a girls' school, you know, I thought it would be better, no distractions except when *I* decided to be distracted. My parents expect . . . no, *I* expect . . . oh, God, I don't even know what I'm *saying*."

Marnie didn't, either. All at once she had a real glimpse of how hard it could be—would be—opening up to people. Sharing what you felt. Listening to what they felt. She thought about curling up in the dirt again, bawling, alone. But that time was past. Past and over.

"You can't know what I mean," Jenna said finally, looking up. Her eyes were very dark. Haunted. "You can't know."

No, thought Marnie. No, not exactly. But . . . she knew enough.

"I know what pain is," she said to Jenna. "And sometimes I feel overwhelmed. There's a lot of . . ." She stumbled. "A lot of . . ." She gestured vaguely.

"Stuff," Jenna said. "Just too much stuff to think about."

They sat in silence, not quite understanding each other, but almost. Almost.

"Listen, we ought to start back," Jenna said. She got to her feet and offered a helping hand to Marnie. "It'll take a while because we'll be walking, but if we go now we'll probably make it there before the sun sets."

Marnie let herself be pulled up. She brushed futilely at the dirt on her sweatpants. Something was nagging her. "Jenna, before. When I was crying. You said something weird. . . ." Marnie frowned, and discovered that she did, after all, remember precisely. She quoted to Jenna, "You said, 'What'll your boyfriend think if you fall apart like this?' and then you said, 'He'll be sorry he ever wrote you that sonnet.' "

Jenna looked a little self-conscious. "So?"

Marnie shook her head. "What sonnet?" she asked softly.

Their eyes met. Jenna was looking acutely uncomfortable. "You left your e-mail on in my room. Remember?" Suddenly she flushed. "You were using my computer! What did you expect? That I wouldn't check out what you were doing?"

"You read my e-mail that night. After I left." Marnie felt like a fool. She'd known at the time it was likely. She had just . . . forgotten.

"No, not then. The next morning." Jenna paused. "I deleted it all after I'd read it, too. There were several messages. Just the one poem, though." Another pause. Then, defensively: "I'm sorry. I was angry . . . and . . . and confused. Well, you know."

Marnie couldn't seem to find anything to say.

"It was a very derivative sonnet," Jenna said, after a minute or two of silence. "My guess is, he'd been reading a little too much John Donne." And then: "Not that there's anything wrong with John Donne. Anyway. I'm sorry."

Marnie said, feebly, "Forget it." She watched Jenna's shoulders sag in relief.

"He'll have a copy," Jenna said. "You can just ask him for it."

Could she? Marnie wondered. Could you ask for a poem that was written for you before the writer really knew you? Would the Elf want her to have it, now that he did know her? He hadn't mentioned the e-mail recently.

Another thought flickered into Marnie's head. "You were the one who told people I might've run off to visit a guy I met online."

"You didn't know that?" said Jenna, surprised.

"No." Marnie flushed. She should have; it was obvious now.

"Let's go," said Jenna tersely.

They began walking. Something still felt unfinished, Marnie thought. Then she knew what it was, and she stopped in the road. Jenna stopped too, and turned, her face apprehensive.

"What now?"

"Just—thanks," Marnie said with difficulty. She cleared her throat and said it again. This time it came out more strongly. "Thank you, Jenna."

After a second, Jenna nodded. Shrugged.

"And . . . I'm sorry," Marnie continued steadily. "For . . . you know. I misjudged you. I was . . . well, wrong. About a number of things."

"Yeah," said Jenna. For a long moment they looked at each other, still wary. "Me too," Jenna said unexpectedly.

They walked the rest of the way back to school together in silence.

CHAPTER
36

Marnie felt unutterably weary. As she approached her dorm room, she wanted nothing more than to throw herself on the bed—without showering, without even undressing—and sleep, sleep, sleep. But when she pushed her open door wider and entered, there was her computer. And Marnie found herself sitting, turning the machine on for the first time since she'd come back. Yes, it was fine; it booted up smoothly. And now she ought to test the Internet connection . . . good . . . and e-mail . . . yes . . .

Nearly two weeks' worth of messages downloaded smoothly into her inbox. Most of them were garbage. Nine of them, in a little cluster, were from the Elf. Nine, not fifteen. So Jenna had gotten into six of them, including the sonnet. But the rest . . .

Marnie felt as if her lungs hadn't begun to recover from her mad run, after all.

I got interested, the Elf had said, when they'd been talking in Leah's basement, just before Marnie noticed that the door was open. . . .

Your boyfriend, Jenna had said.

He's still *interested,* whispered the Sorceress. *More than ever. You know it. Pick up the phone. I bet he left voice-mail today.*

Marnie moved the mouse pointer slowly over the message listings. But she didn't click to open any of them. She closed her eyes, and her weariness overwhelmed her again. She'd fall asleep right here at the desk if she didn't . . . didn't get up . . . and . . .

Just for a minute, Marnie rested her forehead on her arms on the desk.

The Rubble-Eater was dead. All its inarticulate rage and pain finally expended, it lay in a heap on the stone floor of the cavern. Llewellyne stared stupidly at her sword, on which the Rubble-Eater's blood had already begun to darken and congeal.

Abruptly she turned away. She leaned one hand against the cavern wall, closed her eyes, and breathed steadily, but it did no good. She kept seeing the Rubble-Eater deliberately hurl itself upon her sword . . . again, and again, and again. Llewellyne's stomach twisted itself into an impossible knot and attempted to force its way up her throat. For a moment she thought she would choke.

But, said the hawk cautiously, *It was him or you.*

Was it? Llewellyne wondered. Was it truly?

Then she remembered the truth glasses. Suddenly she could feel them, an insistent weight against her

238

chest where they hung on their string. They felt . . . warm. Pulsing. Dread filled her, but she knew she had to put them on.

She fumbled with the glasses, perched them on her nose, and turned back toward the Rubble-Eater. Then, and only then, did she reopen her eyes.

It wasn't the Rubble-Eater there at all. It was a bird, a small hawkling. A baby. And as she watched, it began to stretch its wet, feeble wings. Then it looked up and she could see it fully.

On its head grew crudely bleached, chopped-off hair. And below that were eyes. Defensive eyes. Eyes ringed with black makeup. Human eyes.

Her own eyes.

Above her head, the cyber-construct hawk blinked its own red eyes and suddenly screeched in—fear? rage? No.

In triumph.

And then disappeared.

Startled awake, Marnie groaned. She remembered her dream clearly. She muttered, "Where are Freud and Jung when you need them?" If she really wanted, she supposed she could go into her Paliopolis dreams at great depth with that new counselor. Who, to her surprise, she rather liked.

Still, somehow, she didn't want to talk about the dreams. They felt . . . intensely personal. And, oddly, rather separate from their setting. Whatever they were, they were not about Paliopolis, Marnie thought. Not really.

Speaking of Paliopolis, however . . .

In front of her, the monitor glowed in the near-dark. *You've been inactive for thirty minutes. Do you want to go offline?* it asked. Marnie glanced down at the little computer clock; it read 1:03 A.M. She'd been inactive for a lot longer than thirty minutes. Polite little Internet server, waiting uncomplainingly for an answer hour after hour . . .

She groped for the mouse and clicked No. She was left staring, again, at her e-mail inbox and its list of Elfin messages. Quickly she clicked the e-mail program closed. Then, of its own accord, her hand moved to the Internet browser icon and double-clicked. She had Paliopolis bookmarked. A few seconds for it to load . . . and she was there, at the front gates. Take that, Mrs. Fisher, she thought, but without much malice.

Where are we going? asked the Sorceress.

You know where.

On the way, however, Marnie paused to click through the latest ratings; the Sorceress Llewellyne was still on top, but more than two weeks of inactivity had cut severely into her lead. The Elf had lost ground too; he was way down in the thirties from his previous high of seventeen. She clicked on his name to see if he was currently online, and only after it reported that he wasn't did she realize she'd been holding her breath.

Disappointed? asked the Sorceress. *Maybe he won't be here ever again. Maybe you'll have to check voice-mail . . . or call . . . or see him in person. Maybe this part is over. Isn't that what you want, anyway? Truly? But you're scared . . . and if you're not careful he'll decide you're a lost cause, give up,*

find some smart college girl, some Harvard girl . . .
and all because you're scared.

Shut up, Marnie thought. She clicked over to the list of Paliopolis chat rooms—the Thieves' Den, Throgmorton's Pub, and the Conclave of Magic—and stared at them. Early on, she'd stepped inside the Conclave and listened for a while, but it had just seemed dumb. She'd been interested in playing, in accumulating points, in winning. Not in chatter and gossip.

But . . . were they really talking about her in there, as the Elf—as Frank—had said? Were they wondering, these days, where she was? Why her rating was on the verge of collapsing? She'd spotted an e-mail from the Dungeon Master in her inbox, sent sometime last week; he was probably asking after her.

She was very aware of where she was, physically. In a chair. At her desk. In front of her computer, in her dorm room with its door still slightly ajar . . . at Halsett Academy.

I loved Paliopolis, she thought. It was safe there. But it will never be the same again. It's like childhood. I won't be able to go back. . . .

I know, said the Sorceress sadly.

Marnie took a deep breath. Then, for the last time, she clicked through to the entry chamber, activated her identity and powers, picked up her possessions, and became the Sorceress Llewellyne. It wouldn't take long, she knew, to work her way to the Lair of the Rubble-Eater. She could do it in her sleep. In fact—for a second she wanted to laugh—she had, hadn't she?

241

CHAPTER 37

Methodically Marnie tricked one little guard dragon to sleep, beat three dwarves at poker, and—merely out of habit—exchanged a priceless diamond for an ancient text written in invisible ink. Mere minutes later she stood alone in the caverns below the mountains, next to the shaft that she'd leapt down once before, following the Elf. They'd had a narrow escape from the Rubble-Eater that night. Remembering, Marnie felt her lips move in an almost-smile. The cornered Elf had finally been forced to exchange the spellbook for her grappling hook, and had got himself out of the Rubble-Eater's way only half a second in front of the beast's teeth. Marnie, as the Sorceress, had been laughing so hard she'd actually needed to exchange ten thousand points for a quick resurrection.

Was that the last time she'd been in Paliopolis? She thought it was.

Well. She herself needed no grappling hook. She levitated down the shaft. Reaching the bottom, however, and seeing the screen shift into the familiar graphic, she was immediately aware of disappointment. It hadn't changed; it was exactly what it was supposed to be, and what it ever had been. It was even more familiar since Marnie's dreams. But the graphic held none of the feeling of the dreams. And the Rubble-Eater, a faint rumbling downwind at the left of her screen, held no terror.

There was no hawk anywhere.

Just then another little icon winked into being. *Greetings, Sorceress,* said the Elf.

Marnie found she was not surprised. This, then, was why she had come. And here, at least, she could think of him as the Elf. For a little longer. She typed, *I don't want to game. Would you like to go get a private chat room at the Conclave?*

A pause. Then: *Yes,* said the Elf, and a grappling hook winked into visibility as he pulled it from his pocket. *Right now would be good. Before the Rubble-Eater figures out we're here.*

What's wrong? said the Elf the second they were alone.

Marnie stopped herself just before she clicked Send on *Long story.* She deleted it and typed instead, *I found out some*—she hesitated and then continued—*agonizing stuff about my mother today.* She hesitated again and then typed, *I'll tell you everything another time—if you want me to, that is.*

She stared at the words she'd typed on the screen, wondering if she should send them. If she could

243

imagine talking to Jenna Lowry, surely she could really talk to the Elf? It was different with the Elf. She cared more, and that was dangerous. Maybe she shouldn't . . . maybe she couldn't. . . .

Oh, please. Just click Send, interrupted the Sorceress.

Marnie clicked Send.

The Elf's message came back right away. *Of course I want you to. Meanwhile, are you okay?*

That question again. It was so simple, so ordinary. It took a leap of faith to believe it was genuinely meant.

Leap, said the Sorceress.

No, Marnie typed to the Elf. *I'm not okay.*

His answer came instantly. *What can I do?*

Nothing, Marnie thought. She typed, *You're doing it.*

Doesn't seem like enough.

Of their own account, Marnie's fingers moved. *But what if it's all I want?* She clicked Send even as the Sorceress in her head yelled, *No! Don't!*

The Elf didn't reply for a full minute. Marnie knew because she was watching her computer clock. Finally a reply arrived.

Then I'd be disappointed. You have to know that. Look, I feel like an idiot, but I have to know—did you read all the e-mail I sent you before?

No, Marnie typed slowly. *Someone here at school got into it while I was gone and deleted some of them, and I only just got my computer back, so I haven't had a chance to read the rest.*

She clicked Send, breathed, and then—without permission from her brain—her fingers simply took

244

over the keyboard. *I'm lying,* she typed. *Well, partly. This is the truth: I didn't dare read the ones in my box. I'm afraid to. Jenna—the girl who got into my e-mail while I was away, that part was true—said you sent me a sonnet. She said you'd been reading too much John Donne. I'm not any good at this. Anyway, you wrote those e-mails before you met me. And you don't know me now. Maybe you think you do, but you don't.*

Marnie clicked Send before she had second thoughts, or even first ones. In truth, she had no idea what she'd just said; what it meant. She fixed her eyes on her screen, reread her message, and cringed. It was a confused mess. Just like her. She thought about praying but wasn't sure what to pray for.

Even the Sorceress was silent.

Five full minutes slipped by on Marnie's computer clock. If it hadn't been for the chat room monitor program still showing his name, she'd have thought the Elf had logged off. But he was still there. Wherever "there" was, in this cyber-unreality that was actually so very, very real.

She bit her lip and watched the screen.

Then—segment by segment—an essay appeared.

Okay, Marn, shut up for a while and listen to me. I want to see you in person. I want to GET to know you. We were in serious danger together. Maybe I know you—and you know me—better than you're willing to admit. So I'm going to make a spectacle of myself now. I don't mind that. Okay, that's a lie, I do mind, but I've figured out I can do it anyway and it won't kill me. In fact, I've made a spectacle of myself

245

on purpose so many times I figure I must like it. Only possible explanation. Anyway. Here goes.

I got interested in you weeks ago. A little obsessed, actually. Me and half the guys in Paliopolis. I already told you that. You were like a local legend; you played late and long and you were all business, and okay, there aren't a lot of girls there and gaming guys are pretty desperate, but you stuck out even beyond that. And then you started talking to me; we started hanging out some. It was fun, right? And you were so smart. And then I found out who you were, and that you were my age, and nearby . . . and yeah, I didn't KNOW you, you're right, but you get interested in people before you get to know them. That's how it works, right? Somebody feels compelling. They have some mysterious glamour. This is cyberspace but it's a real place, too. We're both real people. Tell me you know what I'm talking about. Tell me you understand.

Marnie stared at her screen. A minute passed and nothing more appeared. Was he expecting a reply? She read his words over. Cautiously she typed *Yes* and clicked Send. And then—because it wasn't fair to the Elf to keep it back, wasn't fair to let him be all alone in his honesty—she added, *I was interested in you, too. Maybe even a little obsessed. Too.* She clicked Send before she could think better of it.

I KNEW IT, shouted the Elf, and if he'd been physically present, Marnie would have kicked him in his bad leg. But then his essay continued.

So I was fascinated by you, and yeah, I wrote that stupid sonnet and made the mistake of sending it, and

*your friend's right, it was probably pretty bad. I can't
tell you how scared I got, when I thought you'd cut me
off, would never speak to me again. I thought it was
the sonnet; I thought I'd blown it. You probably think
it was insane of me to come looking for you the way I
did. Maybe it was. Stupid stalker behavior. But when
I realized something had happened to you, Marn, I
had to do something. I want you to know, I wasn't
sorry for a minute that I did. Even when I thought we
might die, I wasn't sorry. Because you would have
been alone there, and I couldn't stand even the
thought of that. Even now, it makes me crazy to think
of what it would have been like for you. What it was
like.*

Marnie found herself shaking. She stuffed the
heel of her hand into her mouth.

*And when I really met you—you were such a mess,
and you were so brave. I'm just going to say it, okay? I
fell in love with you. In reality, not in Paliopolis. I
know you don't want to hear it. But I want to say it.
I'm crazy about you. I think about you all the time. It
keeps getting worse. Better. Whatever. I can't believe
you don't feel it.*

"My God," whispered Marnie aloud. "He's not
protecting himself at all. How can he do that? How
does he dare?"

She didn't know.

Are you still there? demanded the Elf.

She took a deep breath. *Yes.*

You want to disconnect? End this right now?

No. And she didn't.

Unbelievable. I'm in a world where NO counts as

encouragement. It could only happen to me. Well, so be it. You want to know the exact moment I fell in love with you?

Yes. Marnie had no memory of actually typing the word and sending it. It just . . . happened. She found that her nose was a mere inch away from the screen. When *had* he fallen in love with her? Was it when they'd gazed into each other's eyes at the bottom of the staircase? Or when he realized she'd poured half their water supply onto his bullet wound? Or maybe it was when they'd lain together on the narrow cot and held hands in silence? Or had it been later, when they'd talked and talked?

It was when you grabbed that bucket of, uh, Yertle.

Marnie blinked once. Twice. She reread the sentence. It said exactly what she'd thought it said.

The Elf had written more. *I thought I would die right there. Die happy. It was the most unlikely Paliopolis fantasy, only real. You just picked up Yertle and went out there to save our lives with it.*

Yertle. Of all things. Yertle.

The Elf was still there. But silent. Time clicked past and Marnie knew he wouldn't write again until she did. He had come much, much farther than halfway. It awed her.

And all she had to do was take a single step. A step she wanted to take . . . wanted . . .

Don't be an idiot, whispered the Sorceress. *Please, please, please don't be an idiot. It'll take some Harvard girl only half a second to snap him up.*

Marnie thought about saying, *I'm crazy about you, too.* It was the truth. She went ahead and typed it. She could feel the Sorceress's urgency. She could feel how much the Sorceress wanted her to send the message. She looked at it and looked at it.

The Elf—no, Frank. Frank Delgado—was still there. Waiting.

Marnie closed her eyes. Just for a second. She put her hand up to her face and discovered it was wet. Then she backspaced over her words, deleting them. She typed, slowly: *Frank? I don't know. I like you . . . but I have some things to work out. It's not you. It's me. I need some time.*

Silence.

Desperate, Marnie typed, *Would you maybe write me another sonnet? About Yertle?*

More silence.

I hate you, said the Sorceress to Marnie. *I just absolutely hate your sniveling, cowardly guts.*

Marnie compressed her lips. It was difficult to breathe. She waited. One minute. Two. Three . . .

And then, after an eon, Frank replied. *Okay. I'm trying to think of rhymes.*

Marnie caught her breath and nearly choked on it. The Sorceress said, *Unbelievable. He's too good for you. Do you understand that? He's too good for you!*

Marnie could hardly believe it herself. *Girdle?* she typed cautiously.

Hurdle. If I drive up, will you go for a walk with me this weekend?

The blunt question startled her, but only for a second. She lifted her chin, as Jenna might have. *Myrtle,* typed Marnie. She sent up a brief prayer and continued: *Yes.* Carefully she added an exclamation point and clicked Send.

And then, startlingly, miraculously, she was

nearly overwhelmed by an intense, unfamiliar feeling. It took her a moment to recognize it. Then she did. It was happiness. And . . . anticipation. And . . . excitement.

Okay, said the Sorceress tiredly. *Whatever. We'll take it.*

CHAPTER 38

Marnie slept deeply for several hours, and it wasn't her fault or her choice that she was wide awake two full hours before dawn, with the vision of the human-eyed hawk vivid in her mind.

She frowned, and then found herself on her feet, swiftly and silently putting on jeans, a thick sweatshirt, sneakers. She touched her amethyst emergency necklace briefly before sliding it under her sweatshirt to lie against her skin. Then she slipped out of the dorm and made her way to the campus quadrangle, where a sweep of lawn made a carpet beneath the early spring stars.

The grass was damp and needed cutting. Marnie sat down in the exact center of the quad. She leaned back and looked up at the stars, which were beginning to fade as dawn approached and the sky lightened.

She thought about Frank Delgado. It was a good name, Frank. It suited him.

They had chatted online for an additional hour last night. Marnie had made him talk about himself, and now she hugged that information close, thinking how much else there would be to discover about him. Like why he'd chosen to deviate from his destiny as a smart, good, preppy boy by dressing like a skinhead. There had to be more to it than what he'd already told her. And she couldn't help wondering—though she could imagine no circumstances under which she'd ask; it was his business, and besides it would help warn pillaging Harvard girls off Marnie's territory—she couldn't help wondering how he'd look with hair.

On the other hand, she liked the camouflage wear. He was so completely uncamouflaged in it.

This weekend, he was going to drive up here. He seemed to think he could borrow his friend's car again. They could go for a walk . . . or, or something. Marnie's body warmed, thinking of seeing him. She closed her eyes for a moment. Would Frank want to kiss her? Would she want . . . oh, yes. She would. She did.

She smiled to herself.

He'd want to talk, too. He was clearly a talky kind of guy. That made her a little uneasy. He'd want to know about Skye, for one thing, and she didn't yet know how to talk about her. Though . . . she had made the smallest of starts on that already, hadn't she, with Frank. And with Jenna—now, *that* was remarkable to remember. Oh, and with Max, of course. And the counselor, even.

Wait! Four people? She had begun talking about Skye with *four* people?

Practically a legion, said the Sorceress dryly.

Marnie shook her head in bemusement.

She wondered what Skye would have thought of Frank Delgado. Skye, who'd had no lover of her own. When Marnie was a child, it had seemed so ordinary, so right, to have Skye entirely to herself. Had it seemed right to Skye? It must have, Marnie thought. Skye was so forceful, so clear. She'd had choices; Max, for one. She had chosen. Marnie couldn't wish for her to have been any different. Skye had flown alone.

"That I should exist at all," Marnie whispered to the fading stars, "is a wonder. A gift. She risked having me, one person who would have to be close . . . when she was afraid of being close . . ."

You learned that from her, said the Sorceress.

Marnie nodded, accepting it.

She helped a lot of people, though, Marnie thought. She saw clearly and wrote about what she saw. With her words she made other people feel stronger, feel supported, in all kinds of ways. Feel loved, even.

That's all true.

I wish she could have loved Max. She must have loved him some, to name him as my guardian. But . . . she couldn't.

If she had, you wouldn't have existed.

253

I would be different. . . .

You wouldn't be you. But you can be Max's daughter now, if that's what you want. It's what he wants, you know that. It's your choice. It always has been.

Marnie's choice. Not Skye's. And not Lea Hawkes's choice. Lea Hawkes, with her secret influence on Skye. Skye had pretended that Lea Hawkes was gone, but she had not been, Marnie saw now. It was Lea Hawkes who had kept Skye alone.

She wondered if Skye had known that. She wondered if Skye had talked to Lea, as she herself talked to the Sorceress.

And now, carefully, carefully, Marnie turned her mind to the other Leah. Leah Slaight.

I am Skye's daughter, Leah Slaight had said desperately. She hadn't been, but in some alternate universe, Lea Hawkes's life might have included a baby while she was seventeen. What would have happened to such a child, born to Lea, not to Skye? That child might have been like Leah Slaight.

Alone. Unloved.

Marnie didn't know what had happened in Leah Slaight's life. She didn't know the experiences and emotions that had led to her delusions. To her need for them. But she found that she wanted to give Leah some kind of understanding, if she could.

Doesn't anyone love you, Leah Slaight? Marnie had asked, in those final moments. She had known the answer must be no. And now, she knew something else. That song—with its bleak lyrics that spoke truth to Leah Slaight and Lea Hawkes both . . . truth about aloneness . . .

It had resonated for Marnie, also. In that kitchen.

254

At that moment. And . . . now. Always. It was the thread of fear that ran through her. That made her want to keep herself apart. That said to do so would keep her safe.

And it lied, that feeling. It lied, because in truth—there was no such thing as safe. Not for anyone in this world.

Marnie sat up and wound her arms around her legs. She watched the first pinkening light. She thought of the little hawkling; wet, scared. She thought of her defenses—of Llewellyne's sword; of her imaginary hatpin. Of all the times she'd backed away from people. She thought of her impulse last night, to back away from Frank. To say no. She had fought it. She would keep fighting, because she knew now what she wanted. She was not Skye, and she didn't believe—would choose not to believe—that being with others would make her any less strong. Or any less herself.

There was no such thing as safety. But—if you dared—you could fly without it.

EPILOGUE

"The funeral is all set for tomorrow, then," said Max on Saturday. His voice on the phone sounded as if he were ticking off items on a list. "The minister said she'd talk to you beforehand about the choice of psalms, so you can pick what you want."

"Thanks," said Marnie. She stood in her dorm room. "See you at dinner, then?" It would be good-bye for now; Max was heading back to New York right after Leah Slaight's funeral.

"Yes," said Max. A pause. "You, um, you've invited your friend to dinner tonight too?"

The Elf. Frank. Involuntarily Marnie smiled. "Yes. He's driving up this afternoon. In fact, I expect him in ten minutes or so. Listen, Max, I think you'll like him."

"We'll see," said Max dryly. "Perhaps when he grows up enough not to need to advertise his indi-

256

viduality quite so loudly . . ." His voice drifted off as he remembered exactly who he was talking to. "Uh, the place I've chosen likes men to wear jackets . . ."

The smile grew on Marnie's face. "Maybe it would be better to go somewhere else."

To Marnie's vast surprise, Max actually chuckled. "Fine. I'll pick you up at seven."

They hung up. Marnie grabbed her sweatshirt and left the building to wait outside for Frank.

She thought of the new, cautious warmth between herself and Max. Of her plans to spend the summer in New York with him and Mrs. Shapiro. Skye would be glad, she thought.

She watched the road. In the following five minutes, six cars passed the entrance to the school, and Marnie realized that she hadn't asked Frank what kind of car his friend had.

Jenna came outside, dressed for running. She waved at Marnie and Marnie waved back. She thought she might take up running. Jenna had offered to coach her, so long as Marnie would promise to follow her instructions exactly.

A maroon Volvo station wagon approached. It wasn't Frank.

A chirpy yellow Volkswagen bug flew right by the entrance to the school.

Several girls walked by Marnie and said hi, a bit uneasily. Marnie said hi back. Might as well. She'd be here next year too, figuring out what she was going to do with her life. Like everyone else.

She frowned and then had to laugh at herself. It was amazing how often she needed to reassure herself that her uniqueness was not in question. She touched the top of her head, where she'd renewed her hair dye. Just in case.

Besides, she liked it.

Another car approached. Marnie tensed. She didn't want to look up, in case it wasn't. She did look up.

Frank was unmistakable, at the wheel of a new, impeccably maintained blue Camaro. If Marnie had been a police officer, she'd have stopped him to see if he'd stolen the vehicle. He parked, sedately, beside the building. How oddly right it felt to see him here at Halsett, in her place.

Marnie walked diffidently toward the car as Frank unfolded his long legs and got out. Just before Marnie reached him, he grabbed a sticklike object from the car and slammed the door.

"Hi," he said.

"Hi."

Marnie was suddenly, hideously conscious that this was the first time they'd seen each other since Leah's death. The first time he'd seen her clean and unbattered.

They stared at each other. Frank's eyes were more incredible than Marnie had remembered. As before, he was wearing boots, camouflage shorts, and a T-shirt, and Marnie couldn't help noticing the neat hospital bandage on his leg. Very different from the one she'd contrived in the basement.

He was looking at her, too. She wondered if he liked what he saw. She'd been careful with her makeup; and she had all her rings on. And the necklace, of course, with the bodyguard on the other end of the electronic link. She put an awkward hand up to ruffle her hair and then pulled it down quickly.

"Nice cane," she said.

"I liked the silver sparkles inside the lucite," said Frank, and lifted it to show Marnie how they floated back and forth in the liquid that filled the cane. Marnie wondered if people were looking at them. She wondered how it would be to have dinner with both Frank and Max tonight.

She wondered how it would be to tell Frank about Skye.

"Wanna take a walk?" he asked. "I need to exercise, and besides, I love this thing." He indicated the cane. Then, as if it were the most natural thing in the world, he held out his other hand for Marnie to take. His face was suddenly serious. Marnie looked at his hand, and, for a moment, she hesitated.

Skye had believed in second chances. In the reinvention of yourself. In the possibility of renewed life, renewed faith. She had written, *The self you invent, the self you live by, that is the self who is important. You are who you choose to be.*

Safety did not matter.

Marnie reached out and took Frank's hand. Their palms clasped warmly. Their fingers intertwined. They began to walk.

She was not Skye. She was Marnie Skyedottir.

Marnie Hawk Skyedottir.

ACKNOWLEDGMENTS

This is the first book that I wrote in an actual office—a place that I love. For the existence of this room of my own I thank my entire family, particularly my sister Miriam Rosenblatt, who told me in no uncertain terms that I needed enough space to get away from myself. If I'm still not *quite* sure what she was insinuating, I'm happy to have been pried away from working in a cramped corner of my living room.

Thanks are also offered to the members of my online writers' group. To those I now know in the flesh and those I still know only in cyberspace—my gratitude for creating a safe, supportive, and very real community in which we can all share our lives and our work. An extra thank-you goes to those who read or heard me read parts of this novel in its first draft. Your thoughtful comments—yes, even the ones suggesting I rethink entire plot strands—were much appreciated once I, um, had had time to consider them fully.

I need to warmly thank my agent, Ginger Knowlton, for the luxurious fact that I never worry about anything she's taking care of.

And finally, as ever, I must acknowledge my very considerable creative debt to my editor, Lauri Hornik. Beyond words, I am fortunate to know and work with her.

Turn the page for an excerpt from

THE
KILLER'S
COUSIN

PROLOGUE

My name, David Bernard Yaffe, will sound familiar, but you won't remember why—at least not at first. Most people, I've found, do not. I'm grateful for that. It gives me some space, however brief. However certain eventually to disintegrate.

When you do remember, it won't be my face you recall. Not that the press didn't shoot plenty of pictures. But it's the photograph of my parents that was famous. That's the one that's developing now in your mind's eye, behind your concentrated frown.

A regular-looking couple in their early fifties. The man thick-haired, blue-eyed. Groomed. The woman's emotions shielded by dark glasses, but her hands betraying her as they clutch the man's coat sleeve, biting through to the arm beneath. His other hand is over hers, comforting—but the man's attention is clearly elsewhere, ahead. Behind them, you can just see the

1

bleak facade of the courthouse in Baltimore on a bitterly cold day.

. The man is looking directly into the camera. I can read his expression, but I defy you to do so. He is practiced at concealing his thoughts, my father. He's a lawyer. A *criminal* lawyer. You'll remember that now, too. Some of the tabloids said it was why I got off. *Behind-scenes wheeling and dealing?* they asked. *Powerful litigator calls in favors?* they hinted.

You'd like to know, I'm sure. Everyone would like to know. But I won't lead you on. This—the story I have to tell—is not about me and it is not about that. I won't deceive you about it, because I am at this moment no more willing to talk about Emily and what happened my senior year of high school—my first senior year— than I ever was.

No, this is about my second senior year. About Lily. Lily, cousin of a killer. My Massachusetts cousin. Lily.

I need to talk about Lily.